Noah Schick

"Noble, worthy, educational, morally uplifting: Barry Yourgrau's *NASTYbook* is none of these things. It's not actually chicken soup for anybody's soul, unless it's the kind of chicken soup that has weird things floating in the depths, and that nobody survives drinking. But *NASTYbook* is very funny, not to mention seriously dark and magnificently nasty, and is thus the perfect book for the budding Count Olaf or Sauron in your family. Or for you."

—Neil Gaiman, author of *Coraline*

"Be warned: these tales are addictive. Read one and you will crave more, and more, and . . ."

—Patrick McGrath, author of *Asylum*

Barry Yourgrau

NASTYbook

JOANNA COTLER BOOKS
An Imprint of HarperCollins*Publishers*

Don't blame just me for this book. Oh no, you must blame Justin Chanda and Joanna Cotler of Joanna Cotler Books. Blame them *spectacularly* (like I do). And while you're at it, go ahead and blame the folks at HarperCollins Children's Books. They're blameworthy—are they ever!—too.

And as for Anya von Bremzen . . . Yes, she tried to stop me, but she couldn't. So I blame her for everything, and now she knows it.

NASTYbook

Copyright © 2005 by Barry Yourgrau

All rights reserved. No part of this book may be used or reproduced in any manner whatsoever without written permission except in the case of brief quotations embodied in critical articles and reviews. Printed in the United States of America.

For information address HarperCollins Children's Books, a division of HarperCollins Publishers, 1350 Avenue of the Americas, New York, NY 10019.

www.harperchildrens.com

Library of Congress Cataloging-in-Publication Data
Yourgrau, Barry.
    Nastybook / by Barry Yourgrau.—1st ed.
        p.   cm.
    "Joanna Cotler Books."
    Summary: Forty-three stories feature such characters as guardian angels who run away from their charges, witches who use the Internet to stalk their victims, and pandas who work as assassins.
    ISBN 0-06-057978-1 — ISBN 0-06-057979-X (lib. bdg.)
    1. Children's stories, American.   [1. Humorous stories.
2. Short stories.]   I. Title.
PZ7.Y8959Nas 2005   2004018412
[Fic]—dc22

Typography by Alicia Mikles
1   2   3   4   5   6   7   8   9   10
❖
First Edition

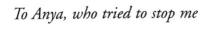

To Anya, who tried to stop me

Contents

Parents

"Luke, we have something, uh, important to tell you," says a boy's father.

The boy is sitting across from his parents at the dining room table. He's been called down here from his room, where he was happily rereading a comic book (*Doom-Kids' Berserk Revenge!*) and sampling from his collection of candy bars.

"All right then, Luke," says the father, looking stern. "No use beating around the bush. Here it is: You're not actually our son. Got it? Today your real parents will come and take you back with them."

"Huh?" says Luke, and he blinks.

"Luke, please don't make this more difficult than it has to be," says the mother.

"But . . . I like it here," says Luke. "I like you guys. You're cool parents."

"Well of course we are!" harrumphs the father. "But haven't you ever wondered why we're slim, handsome, attractive people, full of positive energy and style? And you're kind of a porky, boring schlub, always whining and stuffing your face?"

"My God, do you stuff that face of yours!" says the mother, with a laugh that reflects contempt more than sympathy.

"B-but you're my mom and dad—don't you love me?" blurts Luke, the full horror beginning to dawn on him.

"Didn't you hear? We're not your mother and father!" mutters the father through clenched teeth.

"*Love* you? How could we?" says the mother. She laughs again. "What an absurd idea! I mean, I suppose you're a decent enough kid and all—but—"

"But I like it here. It's my home!" cries Luke.

"Of course you like it, it's a huge, marvelous, well-furnished house!" snaps the father. "We're wealthy and successful people, my wife and I, who wouldn't want to live with us? But the party's over, bud. So go upstairs and get packing."

"No, *wait*—" sputters Luke.

"That's the doorbell," says the mother, standing up. "Must be your real parents now. My, they're early."

A stumpy, dumpy man and a stumpy, dumpy woman come into the dining room and throw their arms around Luke. "Son, it's great to see you again," they tell him, wiping away tears.

After he's given five minutes to pack, they drive him away in a truly smelly old car, with a brief, sudden stop to confiscate and throw out his collection of candy bars. "We don't tolerate that stuff, Ebenezer," he's told. That's his real name, apparently.

Ebenezer.

By evening he's lying numb in his new bedroom, which is a small, airless room in a small, dark, airless house next to a loud expressway. No more comics allowed either.

And that's how suddenly, and chillingly, a person's whole life can change.

Guardian Angel

A man wakes up. It's morning, he hasn't slept well. He's groggy when he steps out of bed and yawns, and stretches. He stretches so fuzzy-brainedly he loses his balance and topples out the window.

As he plummets through midair, his guardian angel runs into the room. The angelic being rushes up to the window, sees what's happening and manages to halt everything just before the man plunges headfirst into the ground.

All this transpires because the guardian angel was off in the bathroom again, with a comic book.

A guardian angel's job is to take care of his assigned person (in this case the man who went out the window). He's not supposed to get distracted reading comics.

And who's ever heard of a guardian angel going to the bathroom?

This goof-off guardian angel now clatters down outside. The fallen man is suspended upside down in midair in his pajamas, two feet above the front lawn—like a special-effects highlight from a sci-fi action movie. It's quite a sight. "He-e-y . . ." the man mumbles dumbly, in a state of acute shock, as would be anyone in his position.

The guardian angel hurries over. Desperately he waves his arms in their flapping angel's sleeves, and blurts a special prayer that will lower the man gently the last few feet to the ground. The angel's heart hammers at this close call. He could lose his job over it!

His heart hammers even harder when he realizes the man won't move.

Further arm-waving and prayer-chanting get him nowhere. Finally the frantic angel just wraps both arms around the topsy-turvy man and tries to yank him down onto the grass. No go. The man is stuck, in midair, in an in-between state of disturbed reality!

By now people have started edging off their porches into the street, gawking at the sight of their neighbor headfirst above his lawn in his pj's.

At this point, even though he's invisible, the angel panics. The actions of a guardian angel in a human's life aren't supposed to resemble bizarro stunts in a sideshow. Such as this humungous, ludicrous spectacle that's going on here.

The panicky angel looks one way, and then the other. And then simply runs off. He high-tails it down the block, around the corner, and off God knows where. Leaving a pile of well-thumbed comic books behind.

Who ever heard of a guardian angel deserting the person in his charge like this? Yet it happens more than most people realize!

After much of the day with perplexed police and firemen on the front lawn, the man is brought down at last, by means of a special crane. The crowd that's gathered breaks into applause, and the shaken man grins, groggily, looking feeble, but miraculously unharmed from his plunge out of the window and his unaccountable midair suspension.

"Must be your guardian angel looking out for ya!" someone tells him, patting his back happily.

"Yeah, yeah," the man agrees, grinning, numb with relief. A pretty misguided and dopey relief. "I guess I got a great guardian angel!" he says, his grin growing wider and wider.

And in this state of ignorance, he embarks enthusiastically on the rest of his life.

Peanut Shells

An elephant desires to improve itself. It manages to get admitted to an elementary school. Then it's caught using cheat notes on a reading quiz.

"Maybe this behavior is acceptable at the circus or at a carnival, I don't know," declares the school principal, grimly.

The elephant looms in front of his desk, its big sheepish head lowered. Reading is a terrible struggle for it, and it sought help in ill-advised ways.

"But it's a no-no here, we won't tolerate it! Furthermore," the principal continues, "we've received numerous complaints about your continuing to eat peanuts in class—leaving your peanut shells everywhere. Eating in class is strictly forbidden!" the principal declares, his voice rising. "We made that absolutely clear when we took the risk and accepted you, against what for some of us was our better judgment!"

The elephant doesn't know what to say. It just shifts about on its enormous elephant feet and mushes its trunk around on the office carpet.

The principal sniffs and lifts his narrow nose. "I'm afraid I have no choice but to expel you," he announces. "This experiment in species outreach is a failure. Kindly turn in your locker key and leave the premises."

The words cut to the elephant's aspiring heart like the knife blade of doom. Its big gray trunk writhes into the air, and it blares in distress. It does so because it's not adept yet at presenting its feelings in an articulate way, which is one of the tools of life that school was to provide, hopefully.

The principal shrinks back in his swivel chair. Not being savvy to the ways of the big top, or the zoo, or the wild, he panics. He lets out a scream, which startles the elephant, so it blares louder.

"Help! Help!" shrieks the principal, giving way completely to alarm. The elephant roars, in a panic now too. It heaves about wildly, this way and that, and crashes into an office armchair and tramples it as it thunders through the doorway and lumbers out into the principal's secretary's office, its big trunk bellowing, its tiny eyes wide with fright. The secretary's shrieks add to the principal's.

Shortly the police race up, sirens wailing. Not having instruction in calming rampaging spooked large animals, they resort alas to unnecessary force. And a terrible mortal tragedy unfolds, with many roars of guns.

The next day all that's left of the elephant's poignant ambitions for self-improvement are some peanut shells that the janitor missed at the back of a classroom. And a page of crude cheat notes for the reading quiz, lifting in the wind out by the trash Dumpster.

And how sad is this: with its skill level the poor elephant couldn't read the cheat notes anyway.

Woodrow

Woodrow has a disturbing insight.

He realizes that pretty much since he can remember, he has felt a strange, constant pressure in the middle of his back.

Uneasily now he turns, and peers over his shoulder—and to his considerable shock, sees the giant wrist of a hand, right there, pressed in under his little checkered jacket! He looks downward: he discovers he is seated on an enormous trousered knee! And above—my God, an immense face is looming over him!

The face talks to Woodrow, smiling the whole time, as if there was something adorable or funny about Woodrow in general. The face poses a simpleminded question:

"So your *family tree* . . . what was it again you were saying? Oak? Cedar? *Number-two pine?*"

Woodrow hears that laughter again, such as he's always hearing, from just beyond the over-bright lamplight of his room. There must be a nonstop party, for heaven's sake, right under his window.

"I never said," he informs the face. "Is that supposed to be a silly joke?" he demands crossly. "Are you getting at something? What ya want from me anyway, *mac?*"

Hoots spill up from beyond the lamplight.

"Now, now, mind your manners, Woodrow," chuckles the face.

How did it know Woodrow's name?

But what startles Woodrow even more is the sound of his own voice. It's high-pitched, in a strained, peculiar, labored way. Somehow it seems not to emerge from himself at all . . . but from the smiling, pressed-closed lips of the face.

A terrible new insight shakes Woodrow like a young tree branch in the wind. "Wait a minute—" he gasps in his eerie voice. "I'm a *puppet?*"

Laughter erupts into applause beyond the lamplight. The face's great eyes gleam approvingly, and there's more delight still, more laughter and applause, as Woodrow twists about stiffly on his perch, his unblinking eyes staring into the anguish of his discovery.

Ghost Story

A ghost decides to get some exercise. Just hanging around, haunting an attic for years and years, can't be so healthy.

It heads off on a nice brisk walk under the moon. It goes down a street of pleasant houses, and turns onto another pleasant street. Dogs rush out barking at first, but quickly they scurry back whimpering into the shadows of their porches, tails between their legs.

The ghost grins. In its earlier life in an age long ago, it was afraid of dogs. But now it strides along cockily, whistling to itself. Then it comes to a halt. It stares up at a glowing second-story window. The chatter and giggling of girls drifts out into the dark night.

The ghost, being a ghost, decides to scare up a little fun.

It sneaks over the painted fence of the house and across to the ivy-covered wall, and starts climbing to the second story.

Inside, behind the glowing window, three girls are having a sleepover. They gossip away in their pj's. The two guest girls offer all sorts of advice about the new braces that their hostess has been fitted with. All at once they turn their heads, in unison, toward the window. They gape.

The ghost grins at them.

"Boo!" it says.

The girls scream and jump up. The ghost waggles its tongue and spreads its fingers by its ears and cries, "Boo!" again. The girls scream at the top of their lungs and clutch each other. The ghost slithers down to the ground and hustles off in the direction it came from. Chuckling merrily.

Back in its attic, however, the spectral being

(let's call it by its formal name) has a change of heart. It begins to feel lousy about its prank. Sure, ghosts will be ghosts. But this ghost has developed a crush: specifically, on the sleepover hostess with the braces. This ghost has never seen braces before. It hovers now in its attic unable to sleep, enchanted by the gleam of a girl's mouth, so silvery, so pretty.

A couple nights later it's back under the second-story window, but this time with sincere apologies. To be offered without causing any fright or alarm. It gazes up at the glowing window, feeling peculiar and light-headed, almost shy. Tonight the lighted window is silent. Good, the hostess must be alone. In bed, maybe reading. Maybe about . . . ghosts? The ghost swallows, truly shyly. It starts ascending the ivy, running one last time over the little speech it's memorized.

Up above, the hostess with the braces sits in bed. Waiting. She's still steamed about being frightened like that a couple nights ago, causing her and her friends to make so much noise her parents threatened to forbid sleepovers for a month! A dreadful sentence she was barely able to whine and charm and beg her way out of.

So she is not all alone by herself.

The ghost reaches the open window. It peers in. It smiles, in an extra-nice, careful, and non-threatening manner. It waves bashfully.

"Hi, remember me?" it begins. "I didn't mean to fri—"

That's as far as it gets. The two guest girls leap from hiding on either side of the window and blast the apologetic ghost in the face with hair spray. This makes the ghost sticky enough for them to grab hold of by its hair and haul inside.

"Creep. *Loser*," the hostess sneers over it in a whisper, as the ghost hacks and sputters on the carpet.

"*Bo-o-o-!*" the guest girls taunt, very quietly.

They have vengeance in their hearts, these girls. They seize the poor spooked spirit once more and drag it over to the closet and stuff it into a bag of dirty gym clothes. Then they lock the closet door, and go about congratulating each other on their trap, being careful to keep their boasting as quiet as possible so the hostess's parents don't start up again.

And with savage delight they review the mischief in store for their dopey intruder. A good laundering in the washing machine . . . with boiling water! Then two extra hours of rinse cycle, two more in the dryer . . . super hot. Then ironing . . . *steam*! Then a nice long drink . . . of *nail polish remover*!

On and on they chatter, and the hostess's silvery braces gleam in such a mean, unapologetic way, it would shock the once-mischievous ghost, if it could see it.

"My Friend Bill"

A lonely boy invents an imaginary friend, a talking bear named Bill. The boy assigns Bill the intimate role of making him feel better about himself.

Every day after school, there in the backyard, Bill waddles up to the boy out of thin air, and sits down in the grass, and smiles lovably, and tells the boy he really is the smartest kid in his homeroom. It doesn't matter what grade he just got on any geometry test. Who cares about geometry, really? And clearly—*clearly*—the boy is also a fine athlete, who could turn around the entire school basketball season, if he cared to, despite his size and flat feet.

And as for *girls* . . .

"You really think so?" whispers the boy, after Bill has named three snotty girls, at the least, who have secret crushes on him.

"Absolutely," declares the bear. And then he scratches his backside and yawns, as the boy stares off grinning at the fence, blushing at this new rosy picture of the world starring his no-longer-lonely self. Courtesy of his imaginary friend.

As for this friend, well, he's lovable, but he's not stupid. Not at all. In fact Bill very quickly gets bored with the sole purpose assigned to him, of absurdly buttering up a lonely young— the word that comes to Bill's mind is "loser." And he grows resentful. Surely there are grander purposes for him being called into being than this after-school nonsense! He can ride a unicycle, if you please, and prance around on his hind legs. Even dance a little. He's got talents.

So one afternoon, when he's summoned for yet another feel-good session in the backyard, the bear says to the boy, "Hey, excuse me one sec?" And he heads off around the side of the house, grinning sheepishly and lovably, as if he was going to go pee behind the rosebush.

But he doesn't. Instead he lumbers off down the driveway and heads away down the road. To find a new and much better life for himself and his talents!

The boy sits in the backyard, pulling at the grass. He scowls impatiently. He's had a bad day. He yells for his fawning friend. He curses the silence. He gets up and stalks over and peers behind the rosebush. His mouth drops open. "Hey . . ." he says. He stares around. "Hey!" he cries. He runs down the driveway. He comes back slowly into the yard, with a kick at the rosebush. He throws himself down cross-legged on the grass and hunches there, scowling in misery and betrayal. Lonely tears prickle down his cheeks.

Out on the wide road, the shadows of evening begin to gather. The imaginary bear trots along, bubbling over with excitement at his bold move, at the adventure he's embarked upon, at the great new world of freedom around him. Sure, he feels a little guilty about deserting the boy—the boy who after all brought him into being. But how much slavish flattery can someone be asked to serve up, day after day after day?

"*Enough already*," thinks the bear.

And he whistles, another of his talents, and skips along merrily in the twilight. Then he hears a curious whooshing behind him in the road, and he turns around, eager for a new experience, and a delivery van runs over him, sending him back to kingdom come. Or wherever he originally came from.

The driver whistles himself, along to the radio, oblivious. The bear was imaginary after all, so visible only to his creator. And now, to no one at all anymore.

The boy feels the pain of Bill's desertion terribly. It's bad enough being scorned by real friends. But by your own personal imaginary friend! Well, that takes the cake. In his pain, the boy writes down the whole candid saga of disloyal Bill, and he turns it in as a class assignment.

I would like to report that, lo and behold,

the story strikes a nerve with other kids in the class. And they become the lonely boy's friends, and they all— But that's not what happens. No, the whole business of imaginary Bill just ends badly, with yawns and lost copies of the story and *I don't get it*s.

So you know what, let's just talk about something else.

Fairy Charm

A fairy loses its balance in a tree, and plunges down right into the campfire of the three campers it was spying on. The campers—startled father and his two young sons—drag the fairy out of the flames. But the little fellow is badly scorched and injured. With his last breath, he begs them to return his bag of charms to his place in the fairy kingdom. Then he hiccups twice and dies.

They bury the dead fairy under the tree. In the morning, they head home. The younger son, Jessie, wants to carry out the fairy's last wish, but his father says no way. It's much too dangerous to get involved in fairy business. They'll just hand the bag over to the police and be done with it.

They arrive home very late. After turning in, Jessie can't sleep. He has a reckless streak, and the idea of an adventure to Fairyland to honor a dying request fires his imagination. Early in the morning, before anyone else is up, he sneaks out of the house with the charm bag.

But where exactly is Fairyland? Jessie has no idea.

Who would? All at once he remembers an old magic bookstore in a dark little alley in town. He's never been in, but surely someone there could help him. If he can find it.

After much hunting, he locates the bookstore and waits outside for it to open, clutching the charm bag, hungry from missing breakfast. At last the door creaks open. Jessie steps inside, suddenly fearful, but also determined.

Deep in the dusty depths of the store, at a dusty desk, sits the proprietor. He has a long beard, and a high bald head ringed with white hair, and more hair sprouting from his long ears. Bold Jessie explains his mission, keeping determination in his voice as best he can.

He holds up the charm bag.

"So how do I take this to Fairyland?" he demands adventurously.

The proprietor stares at him. Slowly, he grins.

"Fairyland? Ha ha," he exclaims. "You'll never get that to Fairyland, you brave, reckless boy. Because I won't let you!" And he roars, and his eyes flash under the wriggling hairs of his bushy eyebrows, and his long beard writhes in strands like a nest of snakes—and a cold wind swirls roaring through the store.

Jessie shrinks back, clutching tight to the charm bag. "Stop—" he stammers.

"Only one thing can save you," cries the proprietor, making his arms dance in the sleeves of his robe. "*Someone who holds the little gold acorn charm in his hand and speaks your name.* But all the fairy's charms are in that bag you clutch to your trembling chest! Ha ha!"

And his laughter swirls and storms through the dusty store, like a terrible wind.

Back at home, the father stands in Jessie's

room with his hands on his hips. "Darn your foolish brother," he says to Jordan, his older son. "Running off with the fairy's bag like this."

"What's that?" says Jordan.

He stoops and picks up a little gold thing from the carpet—he holds it up in his hand. A little golden acorn charm.

"Dad," he starts to say, "I wonder if Je—"

"Stop!" shouts his father. He snatches the charm away. "Don't say another word, for God's sake don't say any names, *you never know what evil spells you can start by accident*! Are you listening? Unlike some other people?"

He wraps the charm in a sock and stuffs it in a drawer.

"Now let's just be rational and get in the car, very calmly, and drive around the neighborhood, I'm sure we'll find that reckless brother of yours," he says.

But of course they never do.

Old&Warty

A witch goes on the Internet to lure victims. She's been around since the Middle Ages, but she tries to keep up with the times.

She logs into a chat room. There she meets a young correspondent named FunkyGal27.

With two warty ancient fingers, the witch types in a simple, but devastating, spell. And then presses "Send," and, of course, cackles.

FunkyGal27's mom becomes concerned about how long her daughter's bedroom door has been shut. "Gretchen?" she calls. "Your father and I made the computer rules very clear, young lady, kindly log off now and come out of there!"

After a long minute, twelve-year-old Gretchen thrusts her head out the door, very exasperated and annoyed.

"*What*, Mom?" she says. "What is the *problem*?"

Actually she doesn't finish her second question, because of the look on her mother's face.

"G-Gretchen—" whispers her mother. "Wh-what are you doing with t-two extra ears on top of your h-head?"

When Gretchen's dad gets home, he logs furiously into the chat room.

"Now listen here, Old&Warty!" he types (that's the witch's user name). "I am FunkyGal27's father. You change my beautiful daughter back to normal—right now, *understand*? Or I'll call the police!"

"Ooh," types back Old&Warty, who's been used to these kinds of threats for centuries. "I am so-o *scared*!"

"You better be!" replies FunkyGal27's dad. "You deranged sicko, *undo your evil*!"

"Just what's so evil about two extra ears?" replies the witch, enjoying herself. "Neh neh," she taunts, "*Fiddlesticks* to you! And *Floppy Ferns* and *Flabby Furballs*—and *See ya later, FunkyGal27's Pater!*" With a gleeful cackle she logs off.

"She's not answering anymore, the old lizard must have logged off," fumes Gretchen's dad. He curses. "God almighty, young lady, didn't we warn you—" He stops, mid-scold. *"What?"* he says. About the way his wife and daughter are gaping at him.

He looks around at the mirror. And he gapes too. His head is covered with eyeballs. Brown ones. Simultaneously they all blink their long lashes.

Then they show off by popping in and out.

The dad screams. His wife and daughter scream.

"Ow *my ears*!" cries Gretchen, trying to cover all four against the noise.

You can bet FunkyGal27's mom doesn't log back into that chat room. The police take down all the information about the outrage, but there's really not much they can do, being cops, not sorcerers.

The family is forced to move to another

state, out of shame. Gretchen and her dad have to wear special ugly medical hats to hide their anatomical "extras." Then they have to switch to medical hoods, to cover their necks and shoulders now too. Eventually their whole spellbound bodies will need covering.

The Internet server shuts down Old&Warty's account as soon as the police call. But of course the witch just opens a new account somewhere else. With a cackle. She finds the cyber age a real hoot and a half.

I'd like to warn you of the new sign-on name she uses. But I dare not, every time I type it I grow another pair of thumbs, to go with the dozen and more I already have.

Panda

A man is lying in bed one evening when a panda bear cub waddles in through the door. The man lowers his newspaper and stares. He stares as the bear climbs onto the side of the bed, upsetting the open box of crackers.

The panda looks exactly like something you'd win at a street fair: black and white, with cute brown eyes and floppy little round ears. Laboriously, it lifts a large ax that you'd use to split wood, and steadies it high above its head in its trembling paws. The shadow of the ax quivers on the newspaper in the man's lap.

The man's lower jaw falls like a dead weight

on his chest. His eyes are as big as golf balls. What hair he has stands up like unmowed grass. He gawks at the raised ax, at the floppy ears, at the cuddly paws wobbling high over the newspaper.

The bear's lips move. *"Sayonara,"* it says.

"H-hey—" the man begins softly. Then he screams. Briefly.

"Monroe!" says a woman, looking up from her knitting. She sits in the living room of the apartment next door. She is sharp featured, severe looking. "Monroe? What was that awful noise?"

At length a boy's voice answers from his bedroom. "I didn't hear any noise, Mother," it whines.

The boy is lying curled up on his bed. He is unnaturally pale. Above his buttoned-up pajamas, his eyes gleam velvety and unhealthy. His cowlick is plastered down on his head, weirdly formal despite the setting and the hour. With a large black pen he slowly draws a line through a name in a notebook. The name is in code; so are the other names listed below. These however still await their decoration by the slow black line.

There is a noise at the window. The boy looks up. The night breeze agitates the curtains. A tubby paw appears, black and white, and feels about for a grip on the sill. It's the panda, returning from its mission.

The boy smiles, dark, strange.

Slave

A kid named Oscar goes to the zoo. He stops at the lion's cage. He stands and looks at the big beast. The lion is lying with a hunk of raw meat between its massive paws. Its shaggy mane puffs out like a giant hairy version of those inflatable travel pillows people put around their necks. The lion blinks its bored, imperious eyes at Oscar. Oscar stares back. Unimpressed. Chewing his gum.

"The king of beasts, huh?" he thinks to himself. "Big deal, he doesn't frighten me. At all. No way."

He blows a bubble and pops it. The lion

36

blinks again at the noise. Oscar chews, and then he gets a very cool idea.

Later that afternoon, Oscar's mother is in the kitchen. It's a nice afternoon out, but here she is cleaning the burners on the stove. Because a certain smart-aleck son of hers (whom we've just met) has gone off without finishing his chores. Leaving her to do this job, rather than heading off somewhere nice and fun herself, like . . . the zoo, for instance.

She hears the kitchen screen door slam behind her and she says irritably, not looking around, "Oscar! Is that you?" Then she turns around, simmering, just as Oscar says, "Hi Mom, look what I brought from the zoo!"

Oscar's mom really doesn't hear his words, though, because she goes into petrified shock. There beside her son, right there in the family kitchen, stands a full-sized lion.

It blinks at her.

"Whatcha think?" says Oscar, grinning coolly, chewing his gum, very pleased with himself. "Man, they have lousy security at that place! Nothing to be scared of," he adds, seeing the look on his mother's face. "He does what-ever I tell him. They call him the king of beasts—but you know what I call him?"

"Dad—" whispers his mother, very softly, her eyes wide as soup bowls.

"Huh?" frowns Oscar. "Not Dad. Slave. I call him 'Slave.' Say hi to my mom, Slave."

The lion blinks.

"D-dad—" Oscar's mom repeats, white as a just-washed napkin. Looking like she's about to cry. *"Dad!"* she squawks.

Oscar observes her and sighs. *"Hey Dad!"* he calls out. "Mom wants you!"

"What?" a voice calls irritably from the living room. The sounds of reluctant footsteps approach. "What's the problem *now*?" grumbles Oscar's dad's voice. Followed by Oscar's dad himself, peering around into the kitchen, peeved, holding the business section of the newspaper.

Followed by him dropping the newspaper. And then him frantically darting in, to grab Oscar's mom, and backing with her out the doorway, in terror.

"You're insane—" he sputters at Oscar. "You're grounded!" he calls back, as he and Oscar's mom go clattering desperately for the stairs.

"Aw, come on!" calls Oscar, going to the doorway. "What's the—geez!" he snorts. "Dad! Mom!"

"You're grounded for the rest of the century!" his father's voice shouts, from the top of the stairs, before his parents' bedroom door slams. There's the sound of furniture being moved.

Oscar turns back into the kitchen, shaking his head. "Of all the—" he mutters. "How uncool can you get? What's the big deal, it's just a prank—what's wrong with that?"

He looks at the lion, which is standing enormously by the refrigerator now. Blinking at him. And starting to think of feeding time.

"What're you staring at, Slave?" says Oscar irritably, snapping his gum, wondering how he's going to get his grounding reconsidered. "See what you got me into, Slave?" he goes on. "Just 'cause everybody thinks they have to be afraid of you. What's to be afraid of? I don't get it."

At which point the lion realizes just how hungry it is now, without its familiar supply of meat. And without warning it opens its jaws, and roars, so the whole kitchen shakes.

And then Oscar understands what there is to be afraid of. "Hey, c-cut that out, S-Slave!" he tells the lion, trying to sneer coolly and be courageous, despite swallowing his gum.

But he's just wasting his time.

Girls' Hockey

A brand-new rookie detective named Harold Muncy gets a case to solve. It's his very first, and it's a doozy.

At the crime scene, Harold finds an octopus lying in the upstairs bedroom. The octopus claims to be the owner of the house, a librarian named Arthur Pincus.

A neighbor had tipped off the police that something "fishy" was going on inside.

"So you're Arthur Pincus, eh?" says Harold, pursing his lips shrewdly.

"That's right," says the octopus, nodding its tall, saclike head, which nestles in the coiling nest of its multiple arms.

"He's lying, the no-good—" snarls the gruff police patrolman who let Harold into the house. "We got a description from the neighbors, Arthur Pincus is a middle-aged—"

"I'll handle this!" says Harold, cutting off the patrolman, who is much older and more experienced, a crusty veteran. But young Harold is the detective.

"So," says Harold, to the octopus. "What d'you say to what the officer here just said? You don't look like a middle-aged librarian to me."

"Sure I do," protests the octopus. "Who says I don't?"

"Of all the—" snorts the patrolman.

"Hey," Harold warns him. "Keep your cool, I said I'm the one running this! Okay then," resumes Harold, turning back to the octopus. "So you're Arthur Pincus, are you? So then tell me: what's the call number for a book on, say—girls' hockey—*since you're supposedly a librarian*!"

"That's easy!" says the octopus. "J796.3, in the Dewey decimal system."

The two cops, Harold and the patrolman, stare at each other.

"Is that right?" says Harold.

"How do I know?" sputters the patrolman. "How should I know about library books?"

Harold goes out to the kitchen and uses the phone to check with the main library.

"He's right," he announces, coming back in. "That is the call number."

"'Course I'm right," snorts the octopus, on a slight note of gloating. "Ask me another one."

"Aw, this is nuts!" complains the patrolman. "Lemme just slap the cuffs on him and take him downtown."

"First of all," replies Harold, "you don't have enough cuffs. And second of all, strange as it may seem, I have to say I think he may be telling the truth."

"You *what*?" blurts the patrolman, in disbelief.

"You can't arrest a man just for looking like an octopus!" Harold informs him, full of the youthful spirit of justice and fair play. "Not in this country!"

"Are you out of your mind?" squawks the patrolman.

"I'll let that remark pass," sniffs Harold.

The chief of police doesn't. He reads the report and immediately orders the octopus hauled to jail, where after eight straight hours of having its suckers tickled, the octopus confesses to being a psychopathic escapee from an aquarium, with an obsession for librarians. Not only has it strangled and eaten Arthur Pincus, it has devoured three other librarians in two different states.

Detective Harold Muncy's career ends right there. He's demoted to junior patrolman and assigned to enforcing overdue fines for the library system. He turns disillusioned and sullen over time, and grows to hate the sight of library books and the voices of librarians. Which is a sad and tragic thing, most people would probably agree.

Ugly

A kid has such terrible skin problems that, in bitter despair, he decides to become a monster.

He drops out of school and makes himself a cave behind the municipal trash dump. There he spends his days berating himself for how ugly he is, and then when night falls and his loathing has twisted into uncontrollable rage, he runs out into the streets of the town, looking for a new home to terrorize.

But being essentially a sweet, growing kid at heart, who just happens to be burdened with a particularly putrid load of zits, spots, pimples, whiteheads, blackheads, and hormonal splotches, he doesn't scream or howl, let alone assault anyone; he doesn't even flash his gruesome face. He just knocks on the panes of dark bedroom windows, and when the sleeper inside calls out, "H-hello? W-who's there?" he squawks, crouching out of sight: "A really *ugly* guy, if you saw me, you'd just pass out!"

Then he runs off.

As pathetic as this behavior might rate on the monster scale, it certainly puts people on edge—plays on their imaginations, gives them an unwelcome jolt when they're still muddle-headed and confused from being unexpectedly wakened.

Then an intrepid girl named Deirdre MacDooley, who's also on the stubborn and haughty side, reads a small article in the local newspaper about this mysterious and annoying "Ugly Awakener." A fan of scary movies, she decides to find out exactly how ugly he really is.

She hides herself, night after night, for weeks, in the overgrown bushes under her bedroom window, lying in wait for the "Ugly Awakener" to strike.

And this is where the story turns bizarre.

Unknown to Deirdre, it's finally occurred to the mother of young scarface that her son has quite a bad skin problem, and he's probably not feeling so hot about life. He's out of the house all the time, she now realizes—probably off somewhere sulking. She's not what you'd call an attentive single parent, this mother, she'll be the first to admit it. To try and make up for her neglect, she leaves a big jar of overexpensive acne cream outside her son's bedroom door, for the next time he comes home.

The kid finds the jar a couple of afternoons later when he slinks back to change his T-shirt and sneakers. In bitter contempt for his mother's inane interference in his personal tragedy, he scoops up an overflowing handful of the medicinal gunk and mockingly plasters it all over his hideous fright-flesh—which tingles a moment, and then clears up, instantaneously, just like that.

The kid gapes amazed in the mirror. He isn't bad looking, actually.

Right away he gives up his fetid cave and his

nightly maraudings and returns to school. He can look people in the eye now, instead of staring at the ground in shame. And he notices Deirdre MacDooley in study hall; and his heart tingles. He even finds the newfound courage to go up and ask her out, awkwardly of course, to the movies.

Day after day he asks; day after day Deirdre informs him, mysteriously, that her evenings and nights are busy right then. "Actually I'm engaged in something *very important,*" she explains, haughtily.

What she's referring to is her ongoing nightly practice of lurking in the overgrown bushes under her bedroom window, waiting to catch a glimpse of the "Ugly Awakener."

Night after night Deirdre lurks, all in vain. Stubborn and intrepid she keeps at it, even when she finally contracts poison ivy, to which she turns out to be grotesquely allergic, particularly around the nose and one of her eyes.

The kid is sweet, but not *that* sweet. One sight of Deirdre's inflamed, scaly, Calamine-smeared nostrils and he turns his attentions elsewhere. He's pretty impolite about it too.

And now haughty Deirdre begins to know what it's like to feel yourself ugly, and shameful, and bitter at the whole laughing world. And she drops out of school and makes her own fetid cave, out behind the sewage-treatment plant.

And this is how monsters are created around us, every day.

Cocoa

"Mom!" says a girl. "I think there's something *really strange* about the foreign exchange student."

This person has just arrived at their house and been shown up to his room.

"Well, he's had a very long bus ride from the city to get here, dear," says her mother. They're in the kitchen.

"But what's with all those weird bandages around his face?" insists the girl.

"Dear, he explained," repeats her mother. "He hit his head when he boarded the bus."

"Mom, you *can't* believe that," snorts the

girl. "And if he's from Norway, how come the skin on his arms is so brown and wrinkled?"

"Why dear, I'm not a dermatologist! Obviously he's a Norwegian who tans easily. Honestly—"

"So how come he doesn't know where Oslo is?"

"Well *gee, Priscilla,*" declares the mother, with that sarcastic note she gets when she's a little vexed and exasperated. "I guess we can't all be the almighty smarty-pants you are! Honestly, Pris," she goes on, "I'd have expected to find a little more of the spirit of goodwill and hospitality on this occasion!"

Priscilla rolls her eyes. *"Mom . . ."*

"Now listen here, Ms. Sherlock Holmes. I don't want another word of all these suspicions. I want you to take this nice hot cup of cocoa upstairs, and knock on his door, *gently,* and give him a nice welcoming smile when he answers. And apologize for disturbing him," she adds.

"Oh, *Mom,*" Priscilla begins again. But with a mother like this, it's useless. She takes the cup of cocoa, turns and trudges away.

Upstairs, in the room, the monster has finally gotten off the bandages around its snout. It stands gasping air, working its reptilian crushing jaws and flicking its tongue over its rows of fangs, which got pressed in painfully by all the facial wrapping. Its trousers are down at its scaly ankles, so its poisonous tail can swish and snap freely. So far so good, it thinks. No real problem getting into the house. Though a brief scare with that girl and her silly geography quiz!

But not to worry.

And now the monster feels again the pangs of its ravenous hunger, and it licks its hideous, slimy jaws. It hums again, high and whiny, narrowing its yellow eye slits. Thinking of all that's out there, right beyond the door. To feed on, *oh yeah* . . .

Out on the stairs, Priscilla comes to a halt. She hears it again, that weird, whiny humming, which she didn't even *mention* to her mom. A voice inside her head starts insisting that things are really *too* creepy, just not good. *Really not good.*

But then she thinks of all the aggravation

from her mother if she goes back down. And she just groans, and starts grimly on up the stairs.

She does pause one last time, right as she's about to knock. But then, gently . . . she knocks.

"Come in!" the croaky, whispery voice cries. *"Yeah, come on in!"*

And I'm afraid that's what Priscilla does. Even managing a trembly welcoming smile, as she turns the handle.

The Werewolf's Garden

A werewolf decides to make a video about himself—a documentary. He wants to tell his story to the world, in his own true terms, as opposed to the hostile and sensationalistic mischaracterizations from which he and his kind have long suffered.

Knowing nothing about the ins and outs of making a video, he hires a budding young director to handle the nuts and bolts of production.

"Wow, what a *cool* project," says the director, tugging at his baseball cap at their first preproduction meeting. "How's about we start with some candid footage of you on a full moon, you know, following you around as you rampage and all—and then we cut the whole thing like a music video, with some slashin' heavy-metal sounds!"

This is exactly the kind of cheap sensationalism the werewolf was trying to correct.

"No no no!" he barks. "I want you to film me in my garden! I'll show the beautiful flowers I've learned to grow, and I'll talk about some of the public service projects I'm supporting, with my own funds, for kids with asthma and such. And I'll reminisce about my childhood, which was surprisingly loving and peaceful, despite my unfortunate condition."

"Hey, you're the man with the money," grins the director. "Just let me say this: speaking as a film professional, I can promise you no one wants to watch a werewolf talk about gardening, they want to see you tearing victims to pieces under a full moon! And howling!"

"Is that so?" mutters the werewolf, flushing dangerously under the ever-present stubble on his cheeks.

"Hey, it sure is!" laughs the director, who

displays a brazen knack for the arrogance of his tribe. "Look—amigo—clearly you don't understand anything about the film biz, so let me—"

"I don't need this," growls the werewolf. "You're fired."

"You can't fire me!" the director chuckles. "Check the fine print in the contract. You think I got no protection here—you think I'd just sign on to some goofball project without rock-solid guarantees against issues of creative differences? You hair-infested schlub!" he hoots, brazen, taunting even.

There's a shocked pause.

The werewolf swarms out of his personalized chair. The full moon is still several days away, but he roars. Blood lust blazes in his crazed eyes. Fangs jut from his lips and claws spike from his grappling fingers.

The director snatches up the video camera and backs away, ducking and filming as the werewolf lunges after him, howling. "Beautiful, beautiful, man!" enthuses the director. "Just stay in focus, stay in focus!"

All his insults of the werewolf have been

planned, you see. He's ambitious, this budding director. He knows terrific things can happen when you take chances, hang it all out—go for it!

But then catastrophes can happen too. Sometimes simultaneously. Sometimes, you can be too clever for your own good. Which is what occurs in this case.

After he's washed off most of the gore and blood, the werewolf decides to shoot his video doc himself. He can fake it through the technical stuff, why not? He has a vision, the werewolf, he'll stay true to it! And he does, like a real artist. He interviews himself in his garden, and films his pretty roses and begonias and offers some asthma tips, and reminisces about his pleasant childhood. And is anybody remotely interested in *The Werewolf's Garden* (as the documentary is called)?

Are you kid—I'm sorry: Yes! Millions are charmed, transfixed! The offbeat doc becomes the surprise box-office hit of the year!

Am I joking? Of course!

But you be the one to break it to the filmmaker.

Strange
Teacup

A hot teen movie star goes to a party. It's one of those notorious wild Hollywood affairs where everyone consumes too much of who-knows-what and pulls a stunt or two that the next day they wish from the bottom of their souls someone had stopped them. At a certain point this movie star drinks from a strange teacup handed to him. He laughs at the peculiar taste. The next afternoon when he wakes up, he discovers he's been turned into a gerbil.

He tries not to panic.

His agent and his publicist, they panic.

"'You loved him as a golden-haired studly

heartthrob'?" squawks the publicist. "'Now you can feel for him as an adorable brown rodent'?"

"'Cuddly, cuddly'?" adds the agent, ashen faced.

"What'm I gonna do?" whimpers the former hot movie star, chomping away in anxiety at a lettuce leaf. "How're we gonna keep this secret? Tell me," he squeaks.

Confidentially, for exorbitant fees, the best doctor to the stars and then the most prominent Hollywood veterinarian are brought in. Neither has a clue. The host of the disastrous party is tracked down and interrogated. He shrugs, shiftily.

"Man, who knows who was there, and what, you know, refreshments they brought with them," he murmurs. Then he grins, happily. "It was one wild ol' night!"

"We'll just have to go public and make the best of it," announce the agent and publicist, grimly. "Better get a little exercise wheel, so you can stay in shape. Don't worry," they add, trying to reassure the distraught former marquee idol, his whiskers a-quiver. "Think of it as a *career move*: the family market. You're gonna knock 'em dead!"

The movie studio is aghast. But they try to make the best of things as well.

"You wanted to elope with him before!" cry the posters. "Now you'll want to steal him from the pet store and bring him home to play with!"

He's Elmo, America's favorite brown pet! (The word "rodent" is a no-no.)

The critics and the audiences don't buy it. "He's not brown, first of all, he's dingy gray," grumbles one influential reviewer. "He squeaks, it hurts your ears!" complain many audience samples. "He's *creepy*," a kid tells an entertainment reporter. "A cute talking mouse is one thing, but with Elmo you want to call the *exterminator*!"

Needless to say, *Our Lovable Elmo* bombs at the box office. There's no talk of a sequel.

"Your career is toast," declare the agent and the publicist. "Maybe some pet shop will take you on to entertain the customers. Can you sing or dance a little? Why didn't you stay away from those wild parties!" they cry, for the umpteenth time.

But who stays away from parties in Hollywood?

The former movie star becomes obsessed with revenge. He dreams in his twitchy sleep of contracting rabies and biting the host of that fateful shindig, repeatedly. Then he gets wind somehow of the next notorious gathering.

He sneaks in, wriggling through a broken basement window. He skitters about furtively through the crowded floors, looking for the host to bite his ankle to shreds, even if no rabies yet. Finally he spots him, on the sofa—and sees him handing a strange teacup to a young movie star: the brand-new golden-haired studly heartthrob.

Suddenly a whole other vision of revenge makes the former movie star break into a diabolical little gerbilized grin.

"Oh yes, yes," he squeaks malevolently, his tuft tail wagging away as he crouches, watching. "Drink it down, golden boy, you drink it all down!"

The young star on the couch gulps down the whole teacupful. "Whoa, that tasted *weird*," he laughs.

"And wait till you see what's coming up," the former movie star cackles, pattering right out into the open. Shrieks go up all around. "It's a rat!" someone cries.

"Nah, it's just that squeaky gerbil, Elmer, from that dud movie," grins the host.

"It's *Elmo*, creep face!" squeaks the former movie star, displaying the vanity of his kind, regardless of circumstances. He rushes toward the sofa, tiny teeth bared. The host swats him aside with a sofa pillow. The star on the couch suddenly screams.

"I'm—*shrinking*!" he sputters.

And before everyone's amazed eyes, right there and then, he shrinks down into another species. A cat.

A blinking, dazed cat.

The gerbilized former heartthrob laughs in glee. "How'd you like it now, gold—" he starts to gloat; but then he squeals. The cat hisses at him. It leaps. And off the two mini former movie stars race in a bloodthirsty chase scene through the party.

The host sits back, chuckling and chuckling.

He shakes his head in admiration over the strange teacup in his hand. "Whoever keeps bringing this teacup, I gotta thank 'em," he declares. "Man," he nods happily, "this is one more wild ol' night of notoriety!"

Orphan

A boy's sister dies. Then his mother dies. Then his father drops dead.

Thankfully, his kindly, saddened grandparents take him in. Then they die too.

Just like that.

The boy gets shipped to an orphanage. A few days later, the institution's dynamic new therapy counselor, whose job it is to size up the newly-alone-in-the-world, goes over the boy's file. He scratches his chin with a pencil, puzzling something out. Then he nods, craftily smiling to himself. He looks up. He smiles at the boy, who sits in an old hard chair across the old, hard desk from him.

"So," says the therapy counselor, a little look in his eye. "You like to *cook*, do you? For *others*?"

"I—I—dunno . . . what you mean," stammers the boy, and sweat breaks out on his low, animallike forehead, under the greasy curiosity of his hair.

"Oh, you don't, do you?" replies the therapist. "Well, how come every one of your relatives died right after you cooked a special spaghetti meal for them? Which you didn't share in, you admit, because you adhere to a bizarre diet of only pistachio nuts!"

And he stares at the boy, smiling like a fox, chewing on the end of his pencil.

There's silence. The boy, whose name used to be Jerome but who's changed it to Dark Lothar, swallows; he blushes.

"Well?" says the therapy counselor, grimly smiling, sucking on his pencil. "What's your answer, young man?"

"Spaghetti . . . was what I used to like to make," murmurs Dark Lothar. "Now I prefer doing things . . . with pencils."

"'Pencils'?" repeats the therapist, lifting a scoffing eyebrow. Suddenly his eyes bulge. "Oh my God—" he sputters, jerking the pencil from his mouth and staring at its oddly discolored chewed end. He flings it away. He starts to shout something, but foam just surges over his lips and he keels over backward rigid in his swivel chair.

Dark Lothar stares at the now empty desk. A violent quiver trembles through his hunched body. Without looking he fumbles out a dirty little bag and undoes all the old rubber bands around it and gobbles down pistachio nuts, one after the other, like a furtive little animal, trembling. Then he redoes the rubber bands and presses the bag deep away into his pocket. Then he turns around, slowly, a grin on his shiny face. He thinks of all the other special pencils he's distributed, all around the orphanage.

And then tomorrow, all around town too, store after friendly store . . . stores halfway around the world, eventually!

"Dark Lothar will rule!" he whispers, and he chuckles and trembles. "Pencils, deadly pencils, spaghetti nevermore!"

His eyes shine with demented light as he creeps away from the therapy counselor's office.

That all the other orphans in the corridor are also creeping along trembling and chuckling with their own little bags of nuts doesn't make an impression on him, at least not yet.

But it will.

Skateboard

At night a kid lies listening in his bed. He listens to the sounds on the roof. Astonishing sounds. There's a slithery screech—like flat fiberglass sliding down a roof angle. Then a pause—then a crunching thud. Like little wheels landing on roof tiles.

Or sometimes a long, bumpy takeoff rumble, straight down the tiles. Then a long pause . . . that never ends.

The sounds are whispery, feathery. Ghostly.

As if there were some kind of skateboarders up on the roof! Whizzing around in the dark, three and a half stories above the ground. But how could that be? Doesn't anyone else in the house notice? Brian (that's the kid's name) decides to go up and check.

He edges out of bed carefully so no one will hear. Stealthily he pads down the hall and then up the attic stairs. And out onto the roof.

In the moonlight, dim slender figures go gliding.

Their dark stocking caps are drawn low over their ears and eyes, their long dark T-shirts flutter over their pale, pale skin. One of them gives amazed Brian a cool thumbs-up, and then jets off across the slope of the roof, catches air over a window gable, hits a lazy 360 turn, lands and rides on down, cutting out finally at the rain gutter. Another kid shoots straight down the tiles, right to the edge—and sails away, out into the trees! Just sails away into the darkness . . .

Brian crouches, shaking his head, laughing in awe. Whoever these kids are, they're masters. Masters.

He watches another one of them blast along, barrel up the side of the chimney, overspin his somersault—and wipe out over the side of the roof. Everyone just looks on and grins.

Brian wipes his sleeve across his lips, swallowing hard. A pale kid glides up and claps him on the shoulder.

"Hey, man, gonna join us tonight, huh?" he says. And he grins in a way that says, "All right!"

Brian grins back, with a shrug. "Didn't bring my board," he explains.

"So what's that?" smiles the kid, and he points. At Brian's skateboard, right there beside him. With a little amazed laugh, Brian takes hold of it. He looks out at the scene around him, and he laughs again, nervously. "Sure looks like an easy way to end up dead!" he gulps. The kid chuckles at this, merry and scornful, so pale under his dark low stocking cap. He cackles something.

"Well?" he then demands. As if to say: Are you just good, or are you great?

Brian takes a deep breath. He springs up and throws down his board and leaps on. His heart pounds as he chutes down the roof tiles, trying to take his place among these masters. He gulps as the rain gutter looms up—and he shoots out, into the night!

His figure seems to hang in space, a silhouette against the face of the moon. It's an amazing ride, an *inhuman* ride. Brian whoops, ecstatically, on and on. And understands now what it means for him, the pale kid's snigger right before he launched:

"Man, how can we end up dead if we're all that way already?"

Tweezers

A young gangster goes on a jewelry heist and when he gets back to his place afterward, he discovers that his ears are gone. Horrified, he wonders if they fell off in the getaway car. He's only newly accepted into the gang, this won't make a good impression.

But they're not in the car. Which is worse, because that means he might have lost them (how do you *lose* your *ears*?) at the scene of the crime, thereby leaving behind evidence for some police doggedness to pounce on.

He can't very well sneak back to the bank to check around. But at least he can wrap a scarf around his head, so his earlessness won't be spotted right away. For a day or two he even wears one of those comic contraptions with pinkish plastic ears on the struts of fake eyeglasses, with a pinkish plastic nose that has a big fake black moustache attached. In other words, a Groucho mask: it looks absurd! He rips it off.

Luckily no mention of ears being found shows up in the papers or the police bulletins. Just as luckily the young gangster doesn't throw away the Groucho mask. Because the next job he goes on, knocking over a convenience store, his nose disappears.

Who knows where it goes, it just . . . *disappears.*

The Groucho mask is not a laughing matter anymore; it's a lifesaver.

The gang of which he is the most junior member starts to get uneasy. There's a note of concern. "So listen, kid," grunts the gang leader, rolling his hefty shoulders. He makes a vague gesture with his big, blunt hands and rolls his shoulders some more. "What's it with all this trouble with your *extremities*? You gotta keep better control of yourself, kid, it don't look *perfessional*."

"Of course, of course, Dainty Dave," gulps the young gangster (gangster bosses have peculiar names, for some reason). "It's just a temporary hitch—maybe an allergy or something!" He laughs, nervously, so his fake nose and moustache wobble. "It's a mystery," he gulps again.

"An allergy?" mutters Dainty Dave. "You wanna see a doctor?"

But the doctor just stares and shakes his head. "It's a *mystery*," he says, and takes a swig from his whiskey bottle.

The mystery continues, unrelenting. Every time the young gangster comes back from another job, another part of himself is missing. *Poof*, gone, God knows how and where. The Dainty Dave gang look grim; they scowl and mutter, all of them now, about "*perfessionalism*." But they're honorable tough guys, which means they grit their teeth and stay loyal. They stick by their mysteriously afflicted young comrade, always in hopes his bizarre condition will straighten out as suddenly and mysteriously as it began.

Eventually the young gangster consists almost entirely of a jumble of fake parts rigged together from toy stores, joke shops, and surgical appliance dealers. He sits balanced precariously in the back of the getaway car; one high-speed bump careening around a curve and he goes clattering all over the seat.

At last all that's left of the real him is a solitary eyebrow. It communicates with the gang by wiggling up and down. At this point the gang takes a secret vote and decide they've gone down the noble route as far as any gangster honor would require. It's time to get rid of him. They're superstitious men, after all; these constantly disappearing body parts are a troubling omen to them, understandably. Time to take that last ride.

The young gangster's eyebrow understands what's in store, it sees the writing on the wall (so to speak). It makes one final request of the gang: that they not employ the torture of tweezers to do their grim job. But such a request is much too subtle to communicate by wiggles up and down.

The pain of each excrutiating *pluck, pluck, pluck*—that, however, wiggling can communicate pretty well, it turns out.

Snip Snip

On Saturday afternoons, while every other kid is hanging out at the mall, or kicking around a soccer ball, or shooting baskets in the drive-way—or just is upstairs yelling at a new video game—one lone boy trudges around his neighborhood, door to door, his head hanging low. His is a terrible fate, right there in the brown paper bag he carries limply by his side.

Inside the bag is a pair of scissors. A little pair of scissors, for cutting nails. Not just any kind of nails.

Toenails.

If some other kid happens to see this boy as

he trudges along his way, he'll grin and maybe snicker a moment or two. Then he'll feel a chill, and a strange sense of awe, and then such relief that it's not him in the boy's shoes. And the adults up and down the neighborhood streets will see the gloomy young figure plodding along, and they'll shake their heads as he goes up to each door and knocks. And they'll sigh as he's let inside.

"Poor young fella," they'll murmur as they wait for him to come knocking at their door. And shuffle inside, and take out his little scissors. And start trimming everyone's toenails.

Big feet, little feet, smelly feet, dirty feet, *really* smelly flat feet; old, yellowing toenails, younger pink toenails, painted toenails, torn toenails. *Snip snip, snip snip*. That's what the poor boy does every Saturday afternoon, whether he wants to or not. (Though could you imagine he ever wants to?) By the time it's almost suppertime, the tears are damp on his cheeks from his terrible labors. *Snip snip, snip snip*. What an awful fate.

And there's nothing he can do about it. Yes,

his desperate parents have spent a fortune on doctors and specialists. "Just a phase," the medical men assure them. "A curious one he'll grow out of." But when exactly, they can't say. And the cause? Can't say either.

"But there's no history of compulsive snipping on my side of the family tree!" protests his father.

"And no incidence of any obsession with toes or feet on mine!" insists his mother.

The doctors shrug, and bow their heads and hold up their hands.

Perhaps it's all a curse. Perhaps a witch or an evil spirit got offended and cast a spell. Who knows; who knows.

It's a riddle and a tragedy. And what if the boy goes on helplessly snipping the rest of his life? Through high school, then college days, then even when he finds a job and he marries and has a family of his own? And every Saturday afternoon throughout the years, there he goes, around the neighborhood wherever he is, with his little pair of—no, it's too awful to contemplate!

Is it any wonder that whenever the boy passes a drugstore with a display of scissors twinkling in the window, he quivers and lets out a scream, and dashes howling across the street, with his anguished parents crying out after him?

Happy Birthday

A monkey wants a birthday party. A real one, with a cake and colored hats and streamers and irritating noisemakers, like the ones the kids who visit the zoo always boast about. The other monkeys burst out laughing.

"A *birthday party*?" they hoot. "Hello, pal? You're a monkey, remember?"

But a couple zookeepers take pity on the monkey. They purchase a cake, out of their own funds, and all the party trimmings too. Actually, they do this not out of pity, but to amuse themselves. It's an exploding cake, you see. They're the sort of zookeepers, rare enough thankfully, who don't mind having fun at a monkey's expense.

The monkey's big day arrives. The primate cage flutters with streamers. Colorful little pointed hats are distributed to all the monkeys, who wear them nervously and shyly, a little overcome with the luxury. Noisemakers toot and squawk. And then the candles of the great banana-crème frosted birthday cake are lit.

At this point the no-good zookeepers edge away from the cage, grinning. The poor unwitting happy monkey takes a huge breath to blow out the candles for its birthday wish. It takes such an immense gleeful breath it keels over backward out of its chair.

So it's on the floor below, out of harm's way, when the cake explodes with such a ferocious roar that it blasts a hole in the bars of the monkey cage.

The monkey immediately hops up and dashes out, while the other stunned primates slowly begin to scream and chatter in the smoke and then leap in all directions, and the zookeepers stagger around in a deafened daze. Everyone spattered with charred yellow frosting.

The monkey races along the roofs of the zoo buildings, until it reaches the zoo gates, where it leaps nimbly out into the top branches of a big shade tree outside. Grinning the whole time! It's a sly monkey, you see. It's known all kinds of zookeepers in its time, and it figured the cake was a trick. So it prepared itself, to take advantage, just in case. And off it races—to freedom!

Happy birthday! Happy birthday!

Happy birthday . . .

This is a dream a poor monkey has, sitting on the dry branch of the tree in its monkey cage.

It sighs. And takes another slow bite of its dusty banana.

And that's our story. It's not a happy one; but then all bananas aren't fresh and golden, and all dreams don't come true.

So the monkey's sad, I'm sad, and you're sad.

Cake

A boy comes into the kitchen at home and sees the cake his mother has baked for his little sister. It's her birthday tomorrow. "Everyone makes such a fuss over her," he thinks. "Last year they forgot my birthday, can you believe it?"

The cake smells chocolaty and wonderful. So wonderful that the boy sneaks a little piece to try. Just a tiny piece, it won't be noticed, it'll hardly ruin the whole cake. And if it does, too bad for his spoiled little sister!

It's delicious!

The boy sneaks a second little bit, a third— a fourth—

By the time he's finally gotten himself under control, only half the cake remains. The boy stares at it, petrified at what he's done. He pushes the cake with its eaten side against the wall, so it appears like part of it is hidden somehow in the wallpaper. But this just looks preposterous.

He decides there's only one way to avoid his family's fury, outrage, and tears at his gluttony. He burps. He'll run away! He's been considering it for a while anyway, what kid hasn't? Now would surely be a good time to do it.

He gets his bike off the porch and speeds off. But he doesn't feel so good, physically, because of how much he's just eaten. His stomach really *hurts*. He swerves over into the neighborhood park and finds a big bush to crawl under, pulling his bike after him. He'll just hide here for a while, rest up til he feels better, and then get going again.

Then he yawns. All that cake, all that emotion, have made him sleepy. His eyelids droop. He starts to nap.

He naps away there under the bush, as the afternoon grows later and later, and evening arrives. His mother comes home and is outraged to find the cake half devoured. So is his father. His sister screams and rushes up to her room and slams the door and sobs at what a selfish brother she has.

Everyone's simply furious at the boy and they don't care that he doesn't show up for dinner. "'Cause he knows what he's got coming!" his mother tells his father.

"And how," says the father. "That greedy, no-good runt!"

The sister just sits quietly, wretchedly sobbing.

Under his bush, the boy sleeps on and on, with his stomach full of cake. All evening he sleeps, and all the long night. He doesn't wake up, not even when the night turns unseasonably cold, and the sparkling frost begins to cover him, like powdered sugar on a cake.

In the morning some kids find him, almost frozen solid. Much too frozen to ever wake up again.

His parents shake their heads grimly in their grief, and murmur, "That's what greediness gets you." They sell off his bicycle at a lawn sale. That's the kind of parents they are; after all, they forgot his birthday last year.

His little sister gets angrier than ever at his selfishness. Because she's now forever known as the sister of the boy who froze to death after eating her birthday cake (the exact percentage of eaten cake gets exaggerated over time). And so her brother really manages to spoil her birthday for the rest of her life. Really, how selfish can you get?

Sandwiches

An escaped convict hides in the old barn at a family's summer house in the country. The girl of the family, named Allison, discovers him when she comes in to read her book in her secret reading place.

"I am a desperate and bloodthirsty man," the convict warns her. "I will pull off your fingers, ears, and toes, and chop what's left of you to sell for bird food—if you tell a single soul about finding me here!"

"O-k-kay." Allison gulps, although privately she reserves the right to tell her summer best friend, Celia Pinkley, who lives down the road.

"Now I am very hungry," says the convict. "And I want you to go in your kitchen and fix me a *sandwich*." And he tells Allison exactly what he wants on the sandwich. Prison food has been a torment for him. In fact it was a major reason for him risking escape. He's been *dying* for a nice big sandwich for years.

"Allison?" says the girl's mother, in the kitchen. "How much are you putting on that *sandwich*?"

"I'm hungry," Allison informs her. As she finishes mounding liverwurst, pastrami, roast beef, ham, peanut butter and jelly, and exactly four slices of pickle, on the sandwich. Then she wraps it up and goes out past her stupefied mother to the barn. She leaves the convict to his feast and scurries away to tell her friend Celia Pinkley her absolutely-no-one-but-*no*-one's-to-know secret.

An hour or so later, the boy of the house, named Alvin, goes out to the barn to gloat privately over his collection of Stars of Martial Arts trading cards. And he discovers the escaped convict. "I am a desperate and bloodthirsty man!"

the convict warns him, with a burp. "And I will pull off your fingers, ears, and toes . . ." etc, etc. All the things he said to Allison; plus how hungry he still is.

"My God!" cries the boy's mother, in the kitchen. "Alvin! What on earth on you putting on that *sandwich*?"

"I'm hungry," mumbles Alvin, as he piles on bologna, roast turkey, American and Swiss cheese, a split hot dog, tuna salad, salami, and exactly four slices of pickle. His mother watches wide-eyed as he wraps up the sandwich and hurries past her out to the barn. She watches him come sneaking out and then run off (to tell his best friend Leonard Starkman his absolutely-no-one-but-*no*-one's-to-know secret).

"Something *odd* is going on over there," the mother tells herself. And with grim purpose she marches right across the badly mown grass to the barn. And discovers the escaped convict, halfway through his second humungous sandwich.

"I'm a desperate and bloodthirsty man!" is what you'd expect the convict to warn. Indeed it's what the convict would like to warn. But instead he just looks at the mother and he moans, bits of pickle and meats on his face: "Ow, I got such a stomachache from all these *sandwiches*." He's in such bad, helpless shape the mother probably doesn't need to grab a shovel and bash the overstuffed convict over the head, knocking him senseless. But she does.

And then the desperate secret about the convict's whereabouts is known to everyone. And the poor escapee goes back to prison. To the torment of that horrible prison food, day in, day out, month after month, year upon year, as if it will never end. All on account of his stomach.

Train

A girl gets on a train. It starts off. Suddenly the girl realizes she's on the wrong one. She rushes to the doors and tries to force them open. A passenger taps her on the shoulder as she struggles and suggests she wait until the train reaches the next station. The doors will then open automatically. The girl realizes the common sense of this suggestion.

She takes a seat and waits anxiously. A long time goes by. The girl begins to sweat. Suppose she is on some kind of bizarre express that only stops at the end of a strange line, miles and miles away? She tries to ask someone for information but the car is filled with too much roaring noise. She lurches to her feet and in unthinking panic pulls again at the doors.

Suddenly the train bursts into daylight. Thundering and screeching, it comes to a halt, its doors fly open, the girl stumbles out onto a platform. She gapes about, dazzled.

A terrifying landscape looms in front of her—glacial cliffs, dark waters, vast plains tormented by wind. The girl lets out a shivering whimper. She turns back dumbly to the tracks but the train is screaming away into the wilderness. The girl screeches and runs pathetically a few steps.

There is a figure on the platform up ahead: the helpful passenger. The girl rushes up to him.

"About every hundred years or so," the passenger replies, thoughtfully, yelling his answer to her question above the wind before he fastens the mouth flap of his billowing parka.

Pizza

A high school kid gets a part-time job at a pizza parlor. He's a delivery guy. His second night a particular order comes in over the phone, and his three coworkers turn around slowly, all together, and grin at him. In an unpleasant way.

"Ooh, you're in for it," says the pie preparer. "You poor sap." And he chuckles nastily. He's a nasty guy.

"Better get yourself some garlic cloves," the oven man tells him, as he hands the order of medium pepperoni to the cash register guy.

Who boxes it up and hands it to the kid for

delivery, saying: "And get yourself a crucifix too." And he winks.

Another nasty guy.

Garlic and crucifixes are what you need to ward off vampires, the kid is thinking as he putters along in his little pizza-delivery mobile. "They're just trying to play with my head, those creeps," he snorts. He turns onto a dark street. It's in a neighborhood of dark old streets. The night has gotten foggy, so he has to squint and peer hard to see the address he's looking for.

It's an old dark house behind tall, mournful trees. The kid's heart is knocking under the logo on his shirt as he gets out of the car, and starts in through a gloomy hedge. He finds himself suddenly hoping the pie preparer put extra garlic on the order. Just in case. Which is absurd, he realizes, and he laughs at himself. Come on, who's he delivering to? *A vampire?* That's just what his creep coworkers are trying to put in his head!

But the sweat is running down from under his paper pizza-parlor hat as he reaches the big, dark, cobwebby front door—and almost drops the pizza as dark wings suddenly brush past him. A bat! Something howls like a wolf in the trees. His knees clack together. He bangs frantically on the door.

"*Ye-e-s-s . . . ?*" a strange, deep voice croaks from inside.

The kid's voice is barely audible.

"P-pizza delivery?" he manages to get out. "It's just a joke, right?" he cries, defiantly. Except his voice is a feeble squawk.

Silence. The dark, cobwebby door creaks slowly open. . . .

"Well, look who's back!" announces the pie pre-parer. The kid comes shuffling into the pizza parlor.

"So you made it," says the oven man.

The cash register guy tilts his head to one side and grins. "*You look awful pale,*" he declares.

The kid shrugs. He grunts something and blinks. He realizes all three of his coworkers are staring at him. He blushes, except his color doesn't change. He feels the itch again.

"Go ahead," says the cash register guy, grinning in a knowing way. "Go ahead and scratch."

"Scratch what?" says the kid, his voice thin and strange.

"Why, the two bite marks on your neck, sonny," says the pie preparer.

"I don't know," stammers the kid, "what you're t-talking about—"

"Oh *yeah*?" says the oven man.

There's an awkward pause as the three coworkers just stand there eyeing the kid in nasty silence.

Suddenly the kid twitches and violently scratches himself. His eyes flare red and he snarls, like a wolf, baring his new fangs.

Whereupon the pie preparer whips out the wooden stake from where it's kept behind the cans of tomato sauce. That's how you take care of vampires, of course: a wooden stake you know where. In this case, right through the logo on a pizza-parlor uniform shirt.

And then the three coworkers sigh, and shake their heads at their nasty practical jokes. And they get ready for the next new kid they're hiring for tomorrow.

* * *

Except the kid vampire got a little coaching from his new master.

That gore around the wooden stake through his shirt? Tomato sauce, as a matter of fact. His chest does hurt, under its special padding. So he grunts in pain, softly, as he sits up in the storage room in back where they've crammed him until they dispose of his body. He reaches up and scratches fiercely at the itch on his neck. His eyes flare red again. He growls, low and eerie, like a stalking beast. He waits, crouching there among the cases of diet cola, the jars of sweet peppers, the sausages, the tubs of Parmesan, the extra aprons. Until he hears the sounds of locking up, the final round of sneering jokes for the night. Then he leaps out and he has himself a little feast. And I do not mean pizza.

Fumes

Unbelievably, a guy scores a date with a girl he has a severe crush on. He's in a state of extreme nervousness as he gets ready. He's a nervous type anyway. He sweats profusely. His personal odor is so alarming he grabs a bottle of his dad's cologne and floods himself with most of it. The odor sinks into oblivion.

"Wow," gasps the girl, slipping into the car outside her house. "You sure smell—nice—" She coughs, nonstop, flapping at the air.

"Thanks," grins the guy, blinking runny eyes from the cologne fumes. "It's nice of you to notice."

The girl looks so awesome he somehow fumbles the keys as he reaches to restart the car, and has to prod around under his feet for them—and this extra delay before they get going, and turn the AC on, allows the fumes to build up to spectacular levels. Cologne and such contain a lot of alcohol, of course, which is highly flammable. "Got 'em!" cries the guy, and he jams the key into the ignition and cranks it, which sets off a spark, which ignites the cologne fumes, which explode into a massive fireball that incinerates the car and its occupants beyond all recognition.

This is the dream that jolts the guy awake, gasping, the night before his big date. He's bathed in sweat. The smell is just awful.

In a tangle of anxiety and responsibility, next day he calls the girl up and cancels the date— "for safety reasons."

"Safety reasons?" scoffs the girl's mother. She laughs, that unpleasant way of hers. "What does *that* mean? There's something weird about that boy," she says, "maybe it's for the best he's stood you up."

"He has not *stood me up*, Mother!" the girl snorts. She ranks so much higher on the school social scale than the guy, it's a sick joke to even suggest he "stood her up"!

But still, a cancelled date is a blow to the pride. She soothes it by having a friend slip word to a certain very cool hottie that she might be available after all tonight. And she heads to the bathroom, to begin the happy arts and crafts of making herself irresistible.

"Phooey, look at me *sweat*," she murmurs— thanks to all the emotional turmoil. She wrinkles her nose at the aroma.

"*Safety reasons,*" she snorts, dousing herself recklessly with borrowed floods of her mother's deluxest perfume, thinking again of Mr. Loser's obnoxious phone call.

It makes her want to lock the bathroom door and sneak a quick smoke (which is a vile habit, unhealthy in so *many* ways).

She locks the door; but the little bathroom window to let out the incriminating evidence is stuck shut.

"What the heck, a couple of teeny puffs, I deserve it," she scowls, and she coughs and blinks, from the built-up perfume fumes, as she scrounges around so *unhealthily* for the matches.

Tickle

Playful Fenton tickles his girlfriend and she laughs so hard, she explodes with a bang into many little pieces.

The girl's parents aren't amused. Neither are the police. Fenton, still shocked and grief stricken by this catastrophe (he loved the girl, whose name was Susan), is put on trial for murder.

"I didn't do anything evil," he protests in his defense. "In fact, the opposite: I just tickled Susan, which is a fun thing people have been doing to each other since forever!"

The judge frowns scornfully.

"You 'just tickled Susan' . . ." he says, clearly

finding this too much to believe. "Okay, you get up and you demonstrate on me how you tickled Susan."

"You sure you want me to?" Fenton answers, looking alarmed. "I mean, what if the same thing—"

"Get up and tickle me!" the judge instructs, sternly.

Fenton shrugs and goes around to the bench, where the judge sits at the front of the courtroom.

"This is all I did," he mumbles. And he reaches in and tickles the judge under the arms of his judicial robes, and then on the side of his belly.

The judge twists and squirms, and then he laughs, and then he screams with laughter. There's a terrific bang. Bits of judicial robe and judicial person drift through the air like peculiar confetti.

"Told you so," murmurs Fenton, as everyone in the courtroom stares in horror. Not to mention shock and disbelief.

After this Fenton is shut away in prison for

the criminally insane, for double murder. Which everyone admits is probably unfair, a miscarriage of justice. But two innocent people are dead thanks to him and his tickling. Something had to be done.

In prison Fenton becomes very despondent and hopeless about all that's happened. So much so that one night the guards hear a sudden fit of squirming laughter from inside his cell, then a giggling hysterical screech, "Oh no, stop, stop!" And then another awful *BANG*!

And this whole terrible episode of tickling claims its final life and comes to its sad, grimly amusing end.

Braces

A boy needs braces on his teeth. He's in misery. A girl requires braces on her teeth. She's miserable. Life with braces is a curse, in a world with mirrors to mock back at you and friends to mock you behind your back.

Then the two woeful brace wearers meet, by chance, in the dim part of the library where the wounded like to lurk. Immediately they both cover their mouths with their hands. Then they laugh, shyly, lowering one finger at a time, in recognition. The sight of each other's smile crammed with crud—peanut butter, flecks of lettuce, cornflake pieces—the sight makes their cursed hearts leap.

Almost at once they go on a date. Their eyes sparkle in the moonlight, their scrubbed-as-best-possible braces gleam. It's love at first sight (pretty much). Suddenly their mouths meet in a feverish, clanging kiss—and stay like that.

Braces caught in braces; snagged and locked.

Their parents protest. But the young lovers decline all dental assistance. They refuse to be separated. They giggle together, in tangled delight, carefully, tooth to tooth as a nurse comes in and hooks them up to an IV machine for nourishment, since they obviously can't eat. They will just stay like this, in their never-ending smooch (at least until it's time for the braces to come off).

So theirs turns into the happiest of stories—how romantic can you get?

Except, unfortunately, the boy falls in love with the IV nurse. The heart is a fickle thing, and the nurse, who never has worn braces, is an awful flirt.

But the girl refuses to be parted!

And then come the painful, painful quarrels, the shouts; and the sheer agony, oh so gruesome, you can just imagine.

Chicken

A wizard chips his tooth eating take-out chicken.

This offends him greatly. He may be ancient and wrinkled and sprouting tufts of white hair from his ears. But he's still vain about his appearance, touchy, even, about certain key aspects at least. It's a front tooth that's chipped!

In a huff he marches back to the take-out place. He demands to see the manager. The bored kid at the counter says the manager isn't in. The wizard, his voice rising, informs the kid what has happened with his tooth and the chicken, which he has brought back in its bag as evidence.

The kid looks blankly through thick glasses into the bag, as the wizard thrusts it open right under his nose. Then he looks up blankly at the wizard, who makes an odd and nutty sight now as he pulls back his lip to display his chipped tooth to maximum effect. His cone-shaped wizard's hat tilts askew on his head; around his shoulders his timeworn wizard cloak droops, its zodiacal thingamajigs food stained and faded.

The kid shrugs. "Beats me," he mutters. "I just got here."

That's it. That's all he says: no apologies, no refund offer, nothing.

He goes back to some little tower he's making with ketchup packets.

Naturally, this kind of service infuriates the wizard. His ancient blood boils. He decides to teach a little lesson in customer relations, there and then.

He takes a step back, and draws himself up in his cloak and hat. *"Hocus-pocus!"* he cries.

And he thrusts out a long, bony finger and twirls it in the air, once, twice—

The entire cooking area behind the kid

suddenly jams to the ceiling with chickens. Live chickens—packed in, squawking and struggling. Spraying white feathers everywhere.

The kid looks around at them. He turns back slowly to the wizard, who stands gloating, arms crossed; a sneer on his wrinkled lips. The kid's hand drifts lazily out.

"Abracadabra," he mumbles. "Or I dunno . . . *Abracadu?"*

An unseen force jerks the wizard into the air. It sends him, shouting, sailing over the counter and plunging, cone hat first, straight into the packed wall of chickens.

Only his curly-toed slippers remain visible, flapping among the hysterical, squawking poultry.

Which goes to show, these days you never know where you'll encounter the art of wizardry. Nor who'll be taught a lesson.

The kid grins through his thick glasses. He shrugs. Then he blinks down into the bag the old one brought in, and he helps himself (carefully) to a drumstick.

The Insect Clerk

A new clerk at a clothing store begins to suspect that one of the other clerks he works with is actually an insect. A big one, of course.

For instance, one time the new clerk opens the door to the store bathroom, not knowing the suspicious clerk is inside. The suspicious clerk is at the basin, washing up. Two long, segmented antennae bob from his bare head. He swings around toward the door and his eyes bulge from their sockets on stalks—three eyeballs at the end of each stalk.

"Oops—sorry!—" gulps the new clerk as you do when you discover the bathroom you thought was vacant isn't.

There's a shocked silence. The suspicious clerk suddenly laughs, a strained hysterical laugh. "It's my Halloween mask!" he hoots.

Since it's July at the time, this explanation isn't entirely convincing.

The new clerk now realizes the suspicious clerk always goes around in an oversized wig and a head scarf, and bulky wraparound sunglasses. "'Cause of an eye condition" is the reason given.

He never buys any of the designer sweaters or the baseball caps from the store, even though clerks get 30 percent off.

More incriminating details: whenever anyone even breathes the words "bug spray," the suspicious clerk screams and runs out into the street.

Or he'll argue with flies that come buzzing in through the windows. He'll start shouting and disputing with them, as if they were people.

Customers find all this behavior creepy. So does the store manager. Finally one day, right in front of some off-put customers, he fires the suspicious clerk then and there, just before lunchtime.

"Get out, you're just too . . . *creepy*! *Weirdo!*" he snarls.

The new clerk feels sorry for the suspicious clerk, who's always been fine to him. He takes him to a café, to buy him a sandwich for lunch. But the suspicious clerk only eats the special salad he always brings with him, consisting of bits of grass and smelly brown gunk, which the new clerk would toss in the garbage, himself. So he just sits and listens sympathetically, the new clerk, which is the kindhearted thing in these circumstances. The suspicious clerk moans on and on, What's he going to do? Jobs are so hard to find for someone like him!

At this the new clerk wonders whether he should bring up his insect suspicions now, even though it's a difficult time. But just to settle the matter once and for all. Because he's curious as well as kind. Whereupon the suspicious clerk does it for him! He confesses who and what he is. Yes, and he's absolutely desperate! Slightly stunned, the new clerk struggles to sympathize in an appropriate insect-sensitive way.

"If I were, you know, you," he suggests,

"maybe—maybe I'd go back and stay for a while with my own, you know—people?"

"Yeah? And live around everyone who looks like *me*?" snarls the insect clerk. Obviously he doesn't like what he looks like and who he really is.

He just hangs his head in his wig and scarf, and sobs away wretchedly under his bulky wraparound sunglasses, three streams running down each side of his flat little nose.

The new clerk can't think of what else to say. He just eats his liverwurst sandwich. He wishes that his lunch hour would hurry and end, so he could say good-bye nicely and go back to the clothing store. The whole scene is getting very, well, creepy. People are beginning to look around from other tables because of the sobbing.

Whereupon the insect clerk's woe grows so violent, so miserable, that his wig and scarf slip down. One of his long antennae pops loose and goes *sprong!* right out in public.

The whole café gasps in horror. A horde of flies swarm over, buzzing out of nowhere. The insect clerk starts arguing with them. He wrenches to his feet and the lumpy shawl he always wears falls off and multiple filmy wings swing into view from his back. The new clerk squawks, his mouthful of liverwurst goes down the wrong way.

"Never!" the insect clerk screeches at the flies. "I'll never give up my dream to be a regular person! Never!"

He shoots up into the air and starts whizzing around under the ceiling, chased by the flies. "Never, I tell you! Never!" his desperate voice can be heard screaming, over the pandemonium below.

Super Heroics

A martial arts superhero starts to lose his powers. He discovers this alarming state of affairs when he intervenes in a bank robbery, an act of heroics that's his stock-in-trade. Except this time when he yells and winds up to deliver his signature flying midair chop-kick of fury, something goes *twinge!* in his back and he just totters off-balance headfirst into the armed robber's stomach, and gets a vicious whack on the skull for his efforts. "Gee, thanks anyway, for trying," mumbles the bank manager, staring at his empty safe.

Empty safes don't look good for a crime-fighting superhero. There's another *twinge!*, another empty safe next time too. "Gee, guess you're losing it, huh?" mutters this bank manager.

The superhero sits at home, and broods. He quits going to the gym to train, because he just limps home now, sore in all his muscles. He looks in the mirror. He sees gray hairs.

"That's it," he thinks, in gloomy distress. "I'm over the hill!"

He loses self-discipline altogether, shocking for a superhero. His diet goes to pot. Flab forms. Now he can't go near the mirror anymore. He just sits day and night, slumped and chubbifying, feeling sorry for his former super-heroic self while he shoves down greasy junk food, which makes him fart all the time, nonstop.

Then one day he wakes up and decides: "That's it, I've hit the bottom of my despair!" A last spark of self-respect flames up in him. He digs out his old martial arts superhero outfit from under the dirty laundry. Some seams split, but it still fits, more or less, by leaving a couple buttons undone. He ties on his black scarf mask. He feels the old blood flowing anew as he turns on his police-radio scanner, and heads out to a bank heist in progress. He's on a mission to rescue his reputation!

At the bank the alarm is wailing, a pair of desperados hectically cram dollars into sacks, brandishing their weapons.

"*Stop!*" cries the superhero. He comes wheezing and huffing through the front door. With a panting, fearsome cry he spins forward, and his knee pops and he sinks, flopping ludicrously, down onto the floor. The robbers gape. Then they burst out laughing. The humiliated superhero struggles to get to his feet and in doing so he lets out a tremendous fart—a poisonous, sewage-grade bomb of foulness.

"Suffering *mercy!*" gasp the overcome bad guys. Desperately they flap their hands and weapons, and then wildly they stagger off through the door, coughing and choking. Right into the arms of the arriving police.

"Thank you—thank you—" blurts the grateful bank manager, sounding peculiar because he's holding his nose with all his might.

And so a superhero is reborn, it seems. The

onetime martial artist now just pigs away at junk food—also undercooked cabbage, refried beans, bags of prunes—preparing himself to uphold justice as The Invincible Stinker (or, in foreign translation, "He Who Triumphs Everywhere, Stinking!").

But superhero success has a subtle logic to it. Its requirements are complex, nuanced. There's the human factor to be weighed. Who wants to be saved from crime, if a stupendous and terrifying odor is the price?—an odor that requires weeks to clear out from a confined space, such as a bank vault or lobby?

An awkward, delicate issue, this one. But real for sure, for anyone who works in a bank. Before very long bank managers are frantically helping robbers stuff the money into their sacks, so they can leave the premises before The Invincible Stinker shows up and unleashes his appalling flatulence weapon.

Finally the whole banking industry presents the porky rejuvenated crime fighter with a plaque honoring his heroics—but at the same time requesting his retirement. The police inform him that it's kind of a court order more than a request.

And sad to say, this is how the fighting spirit of one superhero is finally and irrevocably broken.

Oof Oof

A pair of criminals kidnap a teddy bear from the cozy warmth of a little girl's bedroom. They hold it for ransom out in their decrepit hideout in the cold rainy woods.

The teddy bear, being of such goody-goody teddy bear nature, so cheery and sunny in its little butterscotchy furry heart, tries to keep its spirits up in the face of its ordeal. It hums, under its blindfold.

This humming is vastly annoying to anyone in an edgy mood, such as criminals are perpetually in.

"Knock it *off*," growls the leader of the

criminal duo, looking up with a twitch from the ransom note he's laboriously composing.

"Yes, of course, pardon me, sir!" peeps the teddy bear cheerily. "I certainly didn't mean—"

"Cut the *polite* crud, *creep!*" snarls the junior criminal. He stalks over to the corner and delivers several vicious kicks to the teddy bear's plump tummy-tum.

"Oof!" gasps the teddy bear. "Ooh, oof oof!"

Now "Ow! Ow!" is what you'd expect to hear from any normal someone in these circumstances. But the teddy bear is too cutesy-cute for that. "Ooh, oof oof!" it comes out with.

"Did ya hear that?" sputters the criminal kicker to the other, in disbelief. He twitches now too. "Did ya *hear* that: *'Ooh, oof oof'*?!"

"I heard it," snarls the leader. Violent disgust distorts his already misshapen face. *"'Ooh, oof oof'!"*

"Ooh, oof oof!" echo all the voices in the ill-heated hideout, in differing tones.

"To hell with the ransom!" squawks the criminal leader, tearing up the mishmashed note (whose labors had been inflaming his annoyance levels dangerously already). "Let's teach this snooty so-and-so a lesson!"

This is how the minds of criminals work, on short-term impulses. They rush at the teddy bear and grab it up and throw it against the wall. And kick it some more. And squash its butter-scotchy being into the cold fireplace. "Ooh, oof oof!" bleats the teddy bear as they rip away its blindfold and snatch off its brown button eyes, *pop pop.*

"Ooh, oof oof!" bellow the criminals, mock-ing as they tear off one furry brown ear, then the other, then in a frenzy of twisting and wrench-ing, shred their kidnapped bounty into many teddy bear bits.

And the "oohs" and "oofs" are finally over.

"That'll shut up little creepo," pants the criminal leader, gazing over the shocking bliz-zard of furry pieces around the hideout. "Mr. Prissy-Wissy!" And he twitches, his barbaric chest spasmodically heaving.

That night the ghost of the murdered teddy bear appears floating in the snoring darkness over the bunks in the hideout. The criminals

stop snoring and gape up in naked terror. The
consciences of criminals are always uneasy, and
the ghosts of their victims have a particlar effect
on them.

"Don't be alarmed, I want you to know I
forgive you," announces the ghastly, ghostly
teddy bear, in a wavering oh-so-noble voice.
And then it smiles, eyeless still but somehow
mischievous now, in an aren't-I-so-virtuous-and-
clever way. "On condition you do me a big
favor, okay?" it declares sweetly.

"O-k-k-kay," sputter the criminals, over the
trembling edges over their blankets.

"Just say, 'Ooh, oof oof!'—*respectfully*," says
the teddy bear ghost. "Come on, please. Let's
hear it."

There's a sickened silence in the dark hideout.

"I'm waiting," sniffs the awful butterscotch
specter.

"Oo-ooh," the criminal voices start to bleat.
"Oo-oof oo—" Then they stop.

"*Of all the—*" snarls the criminal leader's
voice.

"What're we, nuts?" snarls the other's.

And the pair of criminals writhe from their bunks in volcanic annoyance and chase the squealing ghostly teddy bear all around the hideout, and finally trap it, and give it such a going over that the little snot nose remembers it for a long time. For all "Ooh-oof-oof-ing" eternity, as a matter of fact.

As for the little girl who owned him, why, she felt the same way about the teddy bear too, understandably.

You'll Find Out

A boy likes to pick his nose.

A harmless habit, a rather human one, you'd think. But whenever his mother sees him at it, she scolds him.

"One day you'll dig out a very unwelcome surprise," she warns darkly.

"Like *what*?" he says, finger you-know-where.

"Stop!" she demands. "You'll find out if you keep that up! And it's *disgusting*!"

"Says who?" says the boy. And he grins. "What's the big deal?"

Things get to the point where his mother

actually sends him to a doctor. The doctor isn't that old, but he looks worn out and haggard, with dark circles under his eyes and pasty anxious skin.

He asks the boy details about his nose-picking habits. The boy answers the questions with a sullen shrug. Then he notices the wads of tissue paper stuffed into the doctor's nostrils.

He grins to himself.

The doctor stands over him, shaking his head. "Man to man," he says— "Man to man, your mother is right, you should listen to her. Awful things will come of this awful habit!"

"That so?" says the boy, boldly. "I'll bet you like to pick *your* nose, doc—you just stuffed all that paper up your nose, so you wouldn't be able to. But you'd like to!"

"No!" cries the doctor. He turns red. "All right—yes!" he croaks. "But I've stopped—but too late, too late for me!"

"What's *that* mean?" grins the boy, and defiantly he reaches up to pick away. Then he freezes.

The doctor is staring at him very strangely.

A violent shudder shakes the medical man. A wad of his nostril paper bursts out. He gasps and shudders again, and a long very thin gray worm, like a strand of overcooked spaghetti, waves out into the air from his nose.

The boy tries to scream, but he's too paralyzed.

The doctor grabs at the nasal intruder with frantic hands. But it's not that easy to seize hold of. The more the doctor fumbles and flaps, the longer and longer the worm grows, slithering from its nostril lair.

The disgusting creature starts to wind around the doctor's head, like one of those long telephone cords that can get you so entangled.

"Call—the nurse!" gasps the doctor, struggling as the worm winds tighter. "Hurry—" He topples back over a chair and thrashes around hideously on the carpet. "Hurry—!"

The boy finally comes to life and runs shouting into the corridor. The nurses rush in and manage to save the doctor. They even chuckle at the whole thing, in a grim way, as they bundle the appalling worm into the medical trash.

"Now don't let all this get to you," the head nurse comforts the traumatized boy, with a smile. "It's a perfectly harmless little pleasure," she whispers, tapping her nose and winking. Then she gives a twitch. She shudders. Frantically her hands jerk up to cover her nostrils, but a little gray head peeps out between her fingers. "It's nothing; ignore it!" sputters the nurse, starting to writhe. "Just ignore it!—"

From that day on, believe me, the boy sticks his fingers elsewhere.

Dark

A boy who's afraid of the dark, let's call him Maurice, goes to stay with his uncle. His uncle lives alone deep in the woods in a dark, old, gloomy house.

"So I hear you're afraid of the dark!" the uncle says to Maurice with a snort at their first dinner, which is by candlelight in the great, dark, drafty dining hall.

"M-maybe a little b-bit," Maurice answers, startled by his uncle's harsh tone. And his peculiar pale appearance.

"Well, we'll cure you of that pronto," his

uncle informs him. "I've put you in the bedroom that's haunted."

Maurice turns pale as a ghost himself. "You h-have?" he says.

"Haunted by a hideous, terrifying ghost, an insane murderer who ripped his victims' hearts out and ate these as they screamed and bled! And was tortured to death himself by the brutal posse who captured him. Torn into little pieces! So what d'you think of *that*?" booms the uncle, his eyes narrowing into sinister slits.

"I—I—" stammers Maurice, barely able to keep from fainting. His horrible uncle seems to swim in the candlelight.

There's a terrible pause. Then the uncle grins.

"Hey, kiddo, just teasing," he says. And he laughs. He sits there laughing, laughing and pointing at the boy. Maurice stares at him, stunned. Then slowly he laughs too. Out of sheer relief, out of the whole crazy, scary scene. The dining room table turns into an uproar of the two of them laughing. The uncle hoots and hoots, he claps his forehead with his hand, in merriment, he throws back his head to bellow with laughter— And his head topples off and bounces on the floor and rolls away. Away into the shadows. And is silent.

Maurice's scream strangles in his throat. "Unc—unc—" he squawks, incoherently.

There's a horrible, stricken silence. Then a strange voice speaks, from deep in the shadows behind Maurice, so his skin turns to ice and his hair tingles.

"Whoops," says the voice. It chuckles quietly. "Oh well, for a dead person he worked well enough for a while." And it chuckles some more. Maurice hears a strange, squealing moan, which he then realizes is coming from himself.

"Why don't you get up and come back here, into the deep shadows?" says the voice. "And bring your *heart* with you."

"D-do I have t-to?" whimpers Maurice, who's been taught to be unfailingly polite, always.

"Oh yes," says the voice.

After a pause, the terrified Maurice gets out of his chair and turns, and moaning, he wobbles slowly into the dark shadows at the back of the great, gloomy, drafty dining hall.

"Poor kid, you're afraid of the dark already," says the voice, sounding very close. "Well, you're going to be afraid a lot worse, I can promise." And it chuckles.

And that's how things work out sometimes, what can I tell you?

Tree House

A kid's mom is nagging him in the kitchen. She's been like this since his dad left suddenly on a business trip.

"Walter!" she says (that's the kid's name). "Another fine summer morning and you're just going out to your tree house again! And why can't you eat your cereal at the table like a normal person?"

"But I like to sit up there and enjoy my ChocoPops," says Walter. Which is the truth. "You wouldn't understand," he adds. Also the truth.

His mom leans forward and squints suspiciously. She shakes a finger. "When your dad gets back from his trip, young man, he's going right up that tree and taking a good hard look inside," she promises.

Walter shrugs. He goes frowning out the back door, and he starts up the ladder carefully, cradling the cereal box, bowl, spoon, and milk in his arms. Carefully he raps on the tree house trapdoor high among the leaves.

"It's me!" he whispers.

Inside Walter's tree house are a pair of spacemen from another world, and their spacecraft. The spacecraft is the real, full-sized, intergalactic thing. As are the spacemen. But they have the capacity to miniaturize their vehicle, so they can work on it after they miniaturize themselves too.

That's how Walter stumbled across them a few days ago, by the back fence.

Now Walter sits in a corner and watches, eating his cereal. "Know how many bowls of ChocoPops I once ate in a row?" he says. "Nine." He burps softly. The spacemen glance at each other in annoyance. Do you how many times they've heard Walter's cereal-bowl boast?

They sigh. They're briefly full-sized again, taking a break from their repairs. They resemble long, silvery rubber chickens.

"Sure you don't want to try ChocoPops just once?" asks Walter, again. And again the spacemen reply, in unison: "NOH THNN-KYEW!"

Their voices sound as if they're speaking through tin cans. They have peculiar accents. "PLAHNETTE UR-THE!" is as close as they've come to Walter's patient naming of where they've landed. They won't say precisely where they're from. They're being extra careful, which is understandable, Walter figures. They just don't know what they're missing with ChocoPops.

Today the spacemen have an announcement: They're leaving that evening. And they present Walter with a gift, in appreciation of his hospitality and his keeping their secret.

Walter accepts a silvery finger ring, made from a curious shimmery metal.

"ITTS SPE-SHUL!" explain the spacemen in their tin-canlike way. They smile, trying not to cackle with laughter. Because what makes the ring so special is the powerful, unpleasant, and permanent odor it will release all over its wearer in a day or two.

But Walter is not exactly a fool. Carefully he puts the intergalactic stink ring in his pocket for now. "Thank you very much," he says.

At dinnertime, Walter sneaks back out to the tree house and carries down the spacecraft and its tiny occupants. He places it in the middle of the lawn as he's been instructed, and then hurries to safety by the house, behind the trash cans. He watches the spacecraft flash into full size for a split second, and then streak away up toward the stars.

He smiles. At some point the spacemen will discover that two of the fuel cells in their intergalactic engines have been replaced with crushed ChocoPops.

"Walter!" cries his mother's voice from the back door. "What's going on out here? Dinner's getting cold! Come inside right this minute, young man!"

"Look," says Walter. And he takes the ring out of his pocket. "I got a present for you."

"Why, it's *beautiful*!" says his mother. Her eyes widen in wonderment. She pushes the ring onto her finger. "What a strange and *lovely* material—it's positively out of this world!" Suddenly she scowls. "Walter, where did you get this?"

"I made it," replies Walter. "Up in my tree house." And he smiles.

"I'll bet," mutters his mother. She har-rumphs.

After dinner, up in his room, Walter opens a bureau drawer. He turns off the light. In the dimness the two spacecraft fuel cells glow like shimmery pieces of chewing gum tinfoil.

"Wonder what'll happen if I put the fuel cells in the gas tank of mom's car?" he thinks. He smiles, and sets his alarm clock for very early, to find out.

Down the hall in his parents' bedroom, Walter's mom slowly removes her face. Underneath, her real face is long and silvery and chickenlike. She tugs off the ring on her finger and opens the closet door. She flips the ring inside, near where what's left of Walter's real mom and dad (who never took that trip) are hanging. Those idiots in the spacecraft probably let the kid with his damn ChocoPops get the better of them. But she will not!

"POO-URR WALL-TURR!" she sneers. In a creepy tin-can voice. She sets her alarm for very early, and smiles as she turns off the light, thinking what's in store for him.

Sibling Rivalry

Two brothers are climbing a big oak tree in the woods, the day before family summer vacation.

Any time you have two young brothers, of course, you've got sibling rivalry.

Each brother is determined to be the one who climbs higher. It's only natural. The younger brother, Philip, finds himself losing. To correct this obnoxious injustice, he gives a little yank at the sneaker of Fillmore, his older brother, above him. Fillmore yells in surprise. And misses his step, and then loses his grip. And just like that he plunges out of control through the branches, hollering past his sibling, and crashes finally to a halt upside down in a bough below.

"My ears!" wails Fillmore. "Help!" He's wedged headfirst into the narrow fork of the bough, his ears scraped raw in the process.

Philip stares, horrified. "It was an accident—" he blurts immediately. To be honest, he also feels an immediate satisfaction that he's no longer the losing climber.

And he has to fight to keep away the giggles, at how preposterous his brother looks, rammed in upside down like that.

Philip shimmies carefully downward, reaches over, and gathers hold of Fillmore's flapping topsy-turvy legs, and pulls.

"Ow! Ow!" the trapped sibling squawks. "My ears!" He's stuck fast.

What to do? "Go get help!" gasps suffering Fillmore.

Philip climbs down all the way to the ground and hurries back along the path. Then he comes past a mound of trash in the bushes, and he stops. He stares in at a thick, faded rope that's been thrown away. All at once he gets a great idea.

He climbs back up the oak tree, ignoring his

sibling's protests about Where's help? "We don't need help," Philip announces scornfully as he starts tying one end of the rope around Fillmore's ankles. "And stop yelling like that," he adds. "Sissy!"

"Not a sissy!" hisses Fillmore.

"Yes you are!"

"Not!"

"Are!"

"Not!"

This is how siblings carry on, I'm afraid.

Finally Philip throws the other end of the rope over a thick branch. Then he climbs down with this end of rope to a very low bough, ignoring Fillmore's questions. And then, clutching the now-taut rope with all his weight, he jumps off. As if he were ringing a big church bell.

There's a terrible scream above him. Fillmore doesn't move for a split second. Then he shoots free, violently upward feet first, and then violently and noisily comes plunging down, landing in a leaf-covered heap on the ground.

His head is missing.

The head remains up in the fork in the

branches. "Ow!" it says. Then slowly it falls loose and bounces down—"Ow! Ow! Ow!"—through the leaves, and lands and rolls to a stop. "My legs—" it sputters. "Can't feel them! My arms! What's going on?"

Philip shrinks back in horror. Who wouldn't? Suddenly he turns and dashes off down the path, fast as he can go, to get as far away as he can from the terrible tree. Then slowly he comes to a stop. Panting, he turns around. And slowly, he heads back toward the ghastly spectacle of his brother. They want to go on vacation tomorrow, after all.

The two siblings arrive home near dinner-time.

"My God, you look so *pale*!" their mother says, seeing Fillmore. His head is back in place. "What happened to your ears?" she exclaims. "And why've you got a T-shirt tied around your neck?"

"He's fine, Mom, fine," Philip assures her nervously.

"Fine . . ." Fillmore repeats, in a strange little voice. "Gonna go . . . shower. . . ."

His mother and Philip watch him, staring each for different reasons, as he shuffles very carefully through the kitchen door, to the hall stairs. He starts slowly up—and then trips and falls on his knees. His head wobbles and topples off and bounces down past him, and rolls into the kitchen.

"Ow!" it says.

"You jerk!" hisses sibling Philip.

Both of them are hard to hear through their mother's screams. She faints heavily onto the kitchen floor.

So the ambulance has two people to take to the hospital when it arrives.

Which is why nobody gets to go on family vacation that summer.

Rope

"So?" says Dad. "How'd it go today?"

The family is at the dinner table. It's the first night of the new school year.

The son shrugs. "Not great," he mumbles into his meat loaf.

"It's his English teacher," says Mom. "He holds class on the roof. It's a sloping roof, it can't be safe!"

"Fiddlesticks," snorts Dad. "They got safety ropes, don't they? We had *all* our classes on the roof back in my day, we loved it. You're just being prissy-hissy."

"Jill Finkelstein lost her balance and fell off!"

sputters the son. "And then she forgot to tie down her books and they almost hit Mr. Feeley, the vice principal, on the head!"

"So they should suspend her." Dad sniffs. "Teach her to be more careful. What's she, still a baby?"

"The poor girl was hysterical from hanging over the side of the building in midair!" replies Mom. "I don't think it's right for a young person to be subjected to that."

"It was *scary*," says the son.

"Oh, *poo*," scoffs Dad. "*Oh, boo-hoo-hoo.* You need to toughen up, Mr. Momma's Boy. That's what education's for. Prepare you for the rough stuff of life, up there in the open air like that."

"Well, I just don't think it's safe," Mom repeats.

"Mom, they're tied with a rope, aren't they?" Dad insists. His tone indicates his patience is wearing out. "Nothing's going to happen to them. Don't you ever listen? Look!" he announces. "Do I have to show you?"

He stands up.

"Don't be silly, Karl," says Mom.

"Geez, Dad—" mumbles the son.

"No!" proclaims Dad. That righteous, condescending look hardens in his eye. "I'm going into the garage, and find some rope, and then I'm going to go up on our roof and you're coming with me and I'm *proving* what a couple of complete wimps you're being about a good old-fashioned educational tool, that's made me the man I am."

And he strides off to the garage, while Mom and the son squawk in protest. At least they protest till he's out of the room. Then they smile at each other, and give an approving nod.

Out in the garage, Dad to his surprise finds a length of rope lying right there, out in the open when he comes in.

He leads everyone up to the roof. He ties a safety knot around the chimney, showing off how easy it is. He doesn't notice some bricks have been loosened. And a few strategic threads cut in the rope. He is lecturing away, "So tell me, how is this unsafe—*how?*" as he lowers himself down the slope of the roof. Contemptuously he jumps off.

So his lecturing words are the last he ever speaks. Unless you count his startled, bellowing scream.

And then the son and Mom are free of that loudmouth harassing know-it-all at the dinner table, forever.

After the funeral, the school year proceeds very nicely. The son turns into a very fine pupil too. All his classes are indoors; which is really no surprise, since classes on the roof were abolished quite some time ago.

Pirate Yarn

A pirate captain all at once becomes violently seasick—all the time. This doesn't go down well with his crew.

How would you feel if your supposedly ferocious leader, Bloody Herbert by name, just lay curled up now in his bunk, limp as a kitten and sweaty and gray, moaning, "Oh, Lordy, stop! Oh, shiver me timbers, won't this dreadful rocking of the ship ever stop!" Just like the worst sort of spineless landlubber.

No, this is not the type of ferocious leadership a pirate crew is looking for.

In disgust finally, they mutiny. But out of

consideration for all the ferocious adventuring shared in the past, they don't force their ex-captain to walk (or in his case now, crawl) the plank, with sharks circling below. They just maroon him on a desert island.

Once on land, of course, Bloody Herbert's seasickness improves instantly. But that's poor consolation for being dumped all by your lone-some on a godforsaken lump of tropical nowhere, in the midst of the empty immense ocean. Bloody Herbert flings off his feathered hat and stamps on it, hopping with both boots. He roars. He curses himself hoarse at the sails of his ship growing tinier and tinier over the horizon.

Then he just sprawls down by a palm tree, pulling his hair and guzzling down the bottle of rum he was allowed to bring with him. Soon he's snoring in a drunken, distressed stupor. His snores rise toward the sun blazing overhead.

In this part of the world, the sun is no joke. When the marooned buccaneer stirs, several hours later, not only is he horribly burned, his brain has actually steamed and swollen in his unhatted skull. He wakes up deranged from sunstroke. For a while he cowers at the base of the palm tree, hissing up at the coconuts, pleading with them to be merciful. Then he struggles suddenly to his feet and prances around, skipping and hopping off balance, chanting nursery rhymes, with a lisp.

This whole distressing spectacle is witnessed by some crabs at the edge of the surf. They decide to take advantage of it, to relieve the boredom of the surf going in, the surf going out, day after day. When the sun goes down, they come crawling out of the water—calling Bloody Herbert's name, which they got off the laundry label on the handkerchief he dropped in his raging. Up the beach they come scuttling and calling, a horde of little hairy things, linking claws and shimmying a little mocking dance in the moonlight as they circle poor sun-baked Bloody Herbert. Who trembles and bellows and whimpers at them behind his eye patch.

And this is where this pirate yarn could easily have ended, there under a marooned moon, teased by seafood. But a shark happens to have kept an eye on all this from out in the waves. And she takes pity on cowering Bloody Herbert. Pity is not an emotion you'd expect from a shark, but this one gave birth fairly recently and feels maternal stirrings amidst her normal savagery.

So she glides in, up onto the beach, and chases the crabs away with a couple of thumps of her tail and gnashings of her terrible rows of teeth.

In his delirious state, Bloody Herbert mistakes her for a mermaid. Hurriedly he retrieves his trampled feathered hat, and readjusts his eye patch, and tramps down to the water's edge. "Ahoy, ye beauteous wench!" he growls. "Come to keep Bloody Herbert sweet company, have ye now? Give us a nuzzle!" And he nuzzles the shark. The shark has never been nuzzled before, and it isn't sure how to react. The pirate captain is surprised at how rough the skin of his mermaid is. "You're a *coarse* one!" he coos, and he pinches the shark.

The shark definitely doesn't like being pinched.

It reacts the way you'd expect from a shark.

Bloody Herbert blinks one-eyed at the gory stump which used to be his cutlass-wielding arm.

"Naughty, naughty!" he chides, gritting his teeth, but grinning. He likes girls who play rough. He gives the shark a slap.

The shark loses all vestige of maternal kindness and devours all of Bloody Herbert right on the spot.

"Naughty . . . naughty . . ." croaks Bloody Herbert's head, inside the shark's stomach. The head manages to grin; but not for too long. The feather of Bloody Herbert's hat tickles the shark's insides—maddeningly. The shark thrashes, and leaps back into the waves, and goes thrashing and bucking and heaving, to make the maddening tickle go away. And if anything can cause seasickness, this would be it.

And so this yarn ends where it began, with Bloody Herbert's whimpers of sickly misery.

Prowl

Late at night, a cat decides to go for a prowl. It slips out of the house. Jauntily it pads along, on the lookout for mice to mangle or another cat to threaten. Suddenly it freezes, motionless, by the yard of the Freeberg residence. Its fur stands on end and its tail rises straight up. It snarls and hisses, not jaunty at all, at the mammoth dark shape slithering around the Freebergs' front porch.

This gigantic shape is a monster boa constrictor.

Slowly it tightens around the porch, cracking the columns, crushing the wicker furniture into splinters, squashing the porch plants into squishy pulp.

The cat gives a last snarl and then backs away and suddenly scurries off down the street. It stops once briefly, to hiss back at the boa constrictor from a safe distance. Then it resumes its prowling, jauntily as it's able, under the full moon. Dark shapes now pass across the moon, like ragged clouds. They're not clouds.

They're pterodactyls from the age of the dinosaurs. Flapping their terrifying leathery wings, squawking with their sinister beaks, they settle onto the roof of the O'Reilly residence. They start peeking at the sleeping windows.

The cat freezes again at this bloodcurdling sight. It hisses and spits now, and one of the pterodactyls turns its beaked head and stares down at it with a hideous, bulging eye. The cat growls sheepishly . . . and slowly backs away, very low to the ground. It scurries off. It dives under a bush and peeps out, whimpering in shock and confusion at the giant dark invaders of its sleeping home street: the crushing boa constrictor, the birdlike dinosaurs.

This unlucky cat, you see, out for a prowl, has somehow gotten caught in the middle of a bad dream that a boy named Sidney Penniforth, who just moved to the neighborhood, is having. Sidney is not a happy kid these days.

The cat decides to forget prowling. It will just head home to its cozy basket in the laundry room at the Sullivans', where it lives. With a feeble growl it slithers out from the bush, and speeds away.

Unfortunately, at this exact moment Sidney Penniforth twists on his pillow and moans and dreams of a horde of crocodiles swarming into the street from the storm sewers, devouring everything in sight. And the squealing cat runs straight into them.

Lake

Two kids go swimming in an out-of-the-way lake. They have it all to themselves. All afternoon they dive, they splash. As it starts to get dark, one of the kids, Patrick, goes into the bushes to pee. He hears a funny loud thrashing in the water. When he comes back out, he gets a shock. Instead of his pal, an ugly reptilian monster (yes, another monster) sits panting on the gray rocky sand. The monster looks around at Patrick and puts on an attempt at a relaxed grin. "Heya," it croaks. It looks ridiculous, trying to pretend everything's normal. It's wearing the disappeared pal's swimsuit around its scaly midsection. Part of an eaten watch strap hangs out from its teeth.

If ever there was a time to panic, this would be it. But Patrick is a very smooth customer. So he just pretends everything's normal too, that he can't tell the difference between his pal and this frightening monstrosity.

"Neat place, huh?" he says.

The monster nods. "Yeah, yeah," it agrees, its voice growling from shockingly deep in its throat. Which sends a chill through Patrick. But he doesn't show it.

"Oh yeah . . ." Patrick agrees back.

This isn't much of a conversation, but it's how he and his departed pal in fact used to talk.

The monster grunts and blinks its scaly eyes in its hideous snout.

It stares at Patrick.

"Oh yeah . . ." Patrick says again. He swallows. "Hey, I wonder how far it is to the opposite shore, wanna race? I'll give you a head start, you go first!"

The monster doesn't move.

"Maybe later . . ." it croaks.

It just sits there. Focusing on Patrick.

There's a long, ominous silence. Patrick gazes straight ahead out at the lake, grinning dopily as if there was nothing on his mind, just the lazy bliss from an afternoon in the water with no one to have to share it with but his 'pal.' The early evening bugs start buzzing around, little black whizzing things. Patrick's mind is whizzing too. Out of the corner of his eye he sees the monster staring away at him, like a vampire, its eyes glowing creepily red. A strange growl starts to swell in its throat. Just to make conversation, trying to cut the tension, stalling for time, Patrick says with a nonchalant laugh, "Gee, getting kinda late, I'm getting hungry, aren't you?" And he burps, like he used to with his pal.

Which is not a smooth thing to do, and have said, under the circumstances. Understandable maybe, but still.

"No, wait, I mean—" Patrick tries hurriedly tries to correct himself. But he's drowned out by a peal of thunder. It's the monster burping too.

"Yeah, I sure am," it agrees. After which there's a brief, frantic scramble, and then another loud thrashing in the water.

And then the monster has the lake all to itself.

Giant Adventure

Three friends decide to sneak into a giant's cave while he sleeps. It's a bold, reckless adventure. Only the foolhardy would ever try it.

The giant's vast cave sits in a hill out past the golf course. An immense hand-lettered sign warns:

PRVIT PRROPTI, STAYY OT!

THS MINS U!!

The adventurous trio slink along the dark cave walls, hearts pounding. They pass greasy mounds of gnawed animal bones, and then towers of rusty old car parts and washing machines, which the giant maybe likes to tinker with, like Lego toys.

At last, beyond dirty socks reeking in piles big as haystacks, they make out a gargantuan shape, looming in the darkness: the giant himself, right there in dreamland!

Thrilled by their deed, and awestruck, the boys break into grins and wild furtive high fives. But only for a moment—because all at once there's a billowing roar. The giant has awakened! A giant lumbering hand begins pawing about, its hairy fingers massive as cattle. The boys scream and try to scramble away. A yellow monstrous single eye glares down over them. One of the boys, Lamont, stumbles and falls. Screeching, he's scooped up and, in one go, gulped down by hairy gargantuan lips.

His two friends, Sandy and Harvey, manage to wriggle inside a gross heap of dirty giant T-shirts. Desperately they cower there, holding their noses at the awful body odor around them, hearing the giant's growling and thudding as he searches on.

At last there's a deafening slow yawn. The cave floor trembles with footsteps trudging back to bed. After a long, terrible burp, the din of snoring starts up once more.

Harvey's eyes are big as saucers. "What'll we tell Lamont's folks?" he sputters. His teeth chatter. "Oh, why did we ever do this?" he whimpers.

"Shut up!" Sandy hisses. "We have to try and rescue him from inside the giant!"

"Huh?" replies Harvey.

"Maybe Lamont's still alive," Sandy points out. "I don't know how we'll do it. Just . . . *climb inside.*"

"That's too *dangerous*!" whispers Harvey.

"Okay, so I'll go alone," Sandy announces. He is the boldest and bravest of the three. "And you're a coward," he adds, to buck himself up.

With a gulp Sandy goes scurrying on tippy toe across the cave floor, to start his heroic mission. First he clambers onto the sleeping giant wrist trailing on the floor. Then up onto the arm, which is like a fallen mighty tree, and then up, up, toward the shoulder. There he crouches, to catch his breath. So far so good! He sets himself, and leaps softly as he can into the hairy undergrowth of the giant's neck. He hand over hands from there onto the giant's chin, and hauls himself past the rumbling, snoring mouth, on up to the giant's nose.

He pauses again, panting. He scans back down the sleeping giant, and off toward the pile of T-shirts in the dark distance, to see if maybe that chicken, Harvey, has somehow found the courage to follow him. Of course he hasn't. With a disgusted harrumph, Sandy turns and climbs up inside one of the giant's dark nostrils.

Far below, deep under the T-shirts, Harvey twists and squirms. "Somebody *please* help," he whimpers. "Oh, why'd I ever let them persuade me to do this?" he moans, forgetting his boastful insistence over the past week.

High above, in the slippery but hairy gusting dark, Sandy squeezes on through the giant's nasal passage. At least he was paying attention for *some* of biology class, he thinks. He starts to giggle at the thought of old Mrs. Schuster, the teacher, as he feels along into a sinus, which is even more slippery and gooey. Suddenly and sharply he drops down through the giant's soft palate, and lands on the back of the giant's tongue.

For one terrifying moment the snoring giant

tries to clear his throat. With a shout, Sandy leaps and wildly clutches onto the overhanging epiglottis with both arms. He swings, back and forth. With a wild brave cry he lets go, and plummets down into the giant's esophagus.

Down and down he shoots, like on a twisting water ride at an amusement park, speeding yelling out of control—until he tumbles out somewhere, and slams right into a big lump of something.

"Ow!" cries the big lump of something. It's Lamont. He's alive! He was swallowed whole by the giant, without chewing. "Oh wow!" Lamont cries when he realizes it's Sandy. He's been lying there shivering, all hope gone. "What a true buddy! What's happened to Harvey?"

Catching his breath, Sandy he tells him all about Harvey. The two friends spend several precious minutes discussing what a pathetic and obnoxious specimen of unloyalty is Harvey Wexner.

"Okay, okay," pants Sandy finally. "So let's get out of here." He's feeling woozy, but pretty heroic about things.

Lamont isn't. *"How?"* he whines. And he looks hopeless again.

They're in the giant's stomach, of course. The route Sandy came in by, the esophagus, is very steep and extremely slippery. Sandy's sneakers slide from under him as he tries to climb a few feet up the stomach wall. And his hands sting. "It's stomach acid seeping in," he cries.

There's only one possible way out: down through the part of the giant's anatomy that's below the stomach.

"I—I can't," protests Lamont. "I'm very sensitive to smells and odors." Which is why he's been just lying there in the stomach, out of hope. "Think of what's down there," he whispers, "what we'll have to go through!"

"We can't stay here," argues Sandy. "The gastric acid'll eat us to bits!"

"I'd rather the acid than crawl through you-know-what's below here," moans Lamont. "Ow! My feet are *stinging*!"

"Come on!" snarls Sandy, tugging at him. "It's our only hope, horrible as it may be!"

He yanks away at his reluctant friend, but

sensitive, hopeless Lamont refuses to budge.

"Coward," hisses Sandy. After all he's gone through to try to save his buddy, he has no choice now but to abandon him. By himself he locates the dreadful hole out of the stomach that is the only path to safety. Holding his nose against what's to come, with the acid now splashing to his ankles, he yells a last time for Lamont, then jumps down into the small intestine.

Unfortunately for Sandy, there is plenty of gastric acid in the intestines, as well as the stomach. So Sandy screams almost as loud as poor Lamont up above him, as he zigzags down toward the waiting horrors of the large intestine, and an exit from the giant—maybe. If he can survive that long.

All this is what happens when three foolhardy friends try to push their luck at a dangerous and ill-advised adventure.

Does Sandy make it? Yes, he does. But his escape route out of the giant's anatomy proves so traumatic that he is never again the lively, cocksure boy he used to be. He twitches all over at bad smells. He mumbles all the time.

And what of sniveling Mr. Chicken, Harvey Wexner? He is rescued, by a posse of dads who come looking when the three boys go missing at breakfast time. The dads take along tranquilizer guns, which they've always had on hand in case someday, God forbid, any of their kids got stupid enough to make giant trouble. A barrage of shots sends the great mean brute back to dreamland, for a long time. Right before he drops off, he burps once, horrifically. Guess who comes flying out? And who's only good from then on for twitching, squealing, and mumbling, himself?

The lone one of the three who can talk is Harvey. After much soap and hot water and hot food, Harvey tells his story: how he climbed in and out of the snoring giant all night, desperately trying to rescue his pals before passing out from exhaustion under the T-shirts!

Sandy and Lamont protest, indignant of course, but everyone just pats them on the back sadly, not understanding a word of their mumbling (or squealing).

So cowardly treacherous Harvey is celebrated thereafter as the hero of this tragic adventure. Wouldn't you know it, in later life he goes on to become a writer.

Alas, a very fine one.

And that, for me, is the other real tragedy here.

Reactor #2

Some catfish are swimming along in their little creek. All at once there's a swell of music, like a choir practicing underwater; a great soft light fills the creek bottom—and an especially golden shaft of this light selects one particular catfish among the transfixed bunch of them, to glow in glory. A deep ethereal voice addresses this fish, in words only it can hear properly.

Then the astounding and awe-inspiring moment is over, and the creek returns to normal.

The other catfish crowd blinking and flicking their tails around the spotlighted one.

"Gosh, oh gosh, what was that, what did he say?" they demand.

The fish that got the star treatment hovers there gulping and gaping. "That was the creator himself, if I h-heard him correctly," it gulps. "And omigosh, he's instructed *m-me* with the knowledge and the m-mission to save all of creation!"

And it gives a trembly little laugh that displays, understandably, shock, disbelief, and pride.

The other catfish laugh too, but not the same way.

"You?—one puny little catfish from Lower Butterberry Creek?" they hoot. "You've been given a mission to save all creation?"

But the chosen fish doesn't seem to hear them. It just stares off into the dim current, as if seeing its epic mission there in a golden haze of glory and immense responsibility. "I must swim upstream," it declares, as if repeating instructions to itself, "upstream farther than any catfish we know has ever swum! And find my way to the governor's mansion, and warn the governor himself to turn off Reactor #2 (whatever that is), *immediately*!" And it stares off, panting.

The other fish stare at it, shocked.

"That's what I must do," gulps the catfish, softly.

There's an awed silence on the creek bottom.

"I must go—I must go at once," the catfish announces, coming back to itself. It gives a shake of its floppy, moustachy whiskers and its fins and tail.

"He must go—he must go at once!" cry the other catfish, bustling this way and that, for want of something to do. The bunch of them form a dense fluttering crowd there by their favorite sunken tree trunk. "God bless you and your fateful journey!" they cry, as the catfish assigned to save all creation flits around and heads off on its mission. "Our hearts and hopes go with you, courage and fortitude to you!" they add.

"Thank you, brothers and sisters!" the chosen catfish calls back, its little heart hammering as it sways away up the creek, straining into the current. It toils around the first bend, and contemplates the daunting odyssey ahead—the miles through forbidding woods, the two thundering waterfalls, the churning shallows of whitewater rocks and swirling pools. And these are just the dangers it knows, all against the relentless current!

But somehow it must *must* flop at last into the governor's mansion, to puff its exhausted, urgent cry: *"Shut down Reactor #2!"*

"Better grab a quick bite, for energy," it advises itself. "I'll be needing every ounce I can get!" It spots an unlucky worm jerking by and snaps it down.

An astounding pain slams its jaws. An astounding force wrenches it up through the water, and out, bursting into air and sunlight.

"I got it, Frank, I got one!" screeches a girl on the creek bank. She jerks around with her bowed fishing rod.

Let history record that her name is Penelope Wilmutter.

"Well bring him in, Pen-Pen, bring him in!" cries her stepdad. Let history remember him as

Frank Finkelmeyer, a pharmacist—at least for one more week.

"Wait, you don't under—I'm on an urgent miss—Reactor # 2—save all creation!" gasps the catfish, flopping about on the rocks where the girl has yanked it. But with the hook through its mouth, all its words are garbled.

"Eek eek, it's flopping about!" cries Penelope, dropping the pole and scrambling away.

"For God's sake, Pen, don't be a baby," mutters her stepdad, "it's one of God's creatures, you gotta put it out of its misery!" Snatching the frying pan from their supplies, he stalks over and bashes the heroic catfish into oblivion, and its awesome mission along with it.

"*Really*, Penelope—" he starts to scold. But then familial considerations take over. "Oh, what the heck, young lady, *congratulations on your first catch!*"

He beams, feeling like a real honest-to-goodness Dad-figure for bonding with his often annoying brat of a stepdaughter over this wonderful Life Moment.

"And wait till we cook this baby up, and you

taste a fish you caught yourself—the first of many to come!" he promises, reaching over and mussing Penelope's hair in fatherly fashion.

Given the circumstances, his promise is positively heartbreaking.

Stars

A girl gazes at the moon out her bedroom window. It's a full moon. It looks so big and close, glowing right there over the top of the maple trees, that the girl leans out and stretches out her arm. To her amazement, she can almost touch the moon. She strains frantically on tiptoe. Almost! She just needs to be a little higher.

Heart hammering, she runs up to the attic and climbs out onto the roof shingles. The moon hangs golden in the sky right above her. She reaches out—she leaps, just like at gym class.

Unbelievably, she's hanging on to it.

"I'm on the moon!" she shouts.

She wriggles about until she's draped on top. She tries to sit up. The moon rocks under her like a big beach ball in a swimming pool.

"*Wow,*" she cries, as she wobbles finally seated upright. "*Wow!*" She stares around open-mouthed at the stars and planets, which sparkle left and right, ahead and behind, so close their individual lights fall on her pajamas like the glow of myriad lanterns.

Suddenly she hears her name called from below.

She looks down. Her father is in his bed-room window. And very angry.

"You get down from there right now!" he half shouts, half whispers, to not waken his wife. "Are you out of your mind?"

"Dad, it's okay," the girl calls down. "It's great!" She laughs in glee and shows off by trying to stand up. The moon sways dangerously and she crouches back down, saying, "Whoops!" She laughs again.

"Stop that!" hisses her father. "Get down, Nadine!" He disappears from the window.

When he reappears on the roof, Nadine looks around hurriedly. An orange globe shines steadily beside her in the heavens. Is that Venus?

"Don't you dare—" warns her father, seeing what she's about to do.

But he's too late, Nadine has leaped over and is clutching onto the nearby planet. Who can blame her when she laughs again? She sees her old man jump himself and grab on to the moon, and holler for her to come back.

But no way Nadine is coming down right now. She peers up at the Big Dipper, right there like a neon sign over her. She leaps for it, and clambers up its handle like a monkey. She looks back and sees her father struggling to keep his moon-top balance. She giggles. She hears her old man's yelling. She ignores it. She spots a starry geometry, which she recognizes all at once from science class. Orion! She jumps at it. And hauls herself up its twinkling legs, and then leaps again, and again, farther and farther, from one glittering constellation to the next.

Yes, until her father's pleading voice has become but a little noise in the distant dark, like a faraway faint alarm, and her home is a dark little spot on the dark globe of the earth. And Nadine is lost eagerly among the stars. Far far away somewhere, deep among the cold, gleaming stars. And no one ever sees her again.

Goblins and
Their Crimes!

A bitter, starving writer of exquisitely arty, bad-selling fiction decides to try his hand at children's books—strictly for the money. About kids and their books he knows nothing.

"But they're hot these days," he thinks. "How hard can it be to make up a story about some little wizard, like what'shisname; or a bunny that runs down a hole? Heck, what about goblins?"

He settles on goblins. He writes his book, enjoying himself, making up all sorts of nasty nonsense, letting off a lot of steam and frustration in the name of entertainment, as writers will do. The book comes out. It's a huge hit. The

Nonsense, it's the book! So turn it over, and start!

community of goblins get hold of a copy.

They're not amused.

"Who be-eth this wise guy, this slanderous clown?" they demand (that's how goblins talk). "Whence come-eth these lies about us being vicious little ugly cowards who steal-eth babies and cast-eth evil spells and go-eth to the bathroom in sleeping families' ears?"

All of which are so-called goblin behaviors brought to vivid life in the pages of the writer's book *Goblins and Their Crimes*!

The goblins call a Gathering among the toadstools in the forest, to determine what to do about this spectacular insult to their good name.

"And he said-eth we never bathe-eth, and smell-eth like dirty piglets!" sputters one little freckle-faced fellow, his pointy ears red with emotion like everyone else's.

The Gathering votes for a firm, but just, lesson to be taught to the offending loudmouth. They will pull out his fingernails, cut off his big toes and replace them with acorns, and make him eat one of his ears in a worms and nettles salad.

"Next time he'll be-eth a *leetle* more careful

about what he write-eth," declares the goblin High Fellow grimly. "Okay, everybody, here be-eth the slimeball's address, let-eth's go-eth get him!"

That evening . . . over at his new duplex garden condominium, purchased with the ill-gotten gains from his book, the writer stands in the French windows of his living room. He's wearing a designer tracksuit and gold chains from his new wardrobe. He swills a crystal glass of outrageously expensive champagne. He chuckles.

"Here's to goblins, the little pests, God love 'em!" he toasts.

He lifts his glass mockingly and then drinks deep (he drinks a lot these days and gobbles away like a glutton, two desserts after most meals, which is why he's turning fat). He sighs and shakes his head happily.

"Next book," he mutters, "hey, I'll make 'em all *drug addicts*—yeah, only the drug they're addicted to is *rancid chocolate milk!*" He cackles at the thought. "This kids' stuff," he gloats. "It's such a *goof*."

He turns his head, hearing something from the

front of the condo. He grins, cocking an eyebrow.

"Giselle, honey bun, is that you?" he coos, thinking it's the glamorous young marketing director from his publisher.

But what's left of her is lying out on the condo front steps. And little bloody figures come swarming and creeping across the front hall carpet— about to change the writer's mood in a hurry.

Or so they think.

But what successful children's writer doesn't have the very latest in security systems, the automatic acid sprays, the motion-sensitive pop-up chopping blades?

"Whoops," murmurs the writer, cringing his shoulders and grinning from the French windows, as he hears the pathetic little shrieks and screams. He flips on the nearby security video screen and surveys the carnage in the front hall, the wreckage on the front steps. "Oh well," he sighs, about the loss of Giselle from marketing. "But what the heck, I'll get the magazines over, there's no such thing as bad publicity!"

And on this cheerful and profound note he goes back to guzzling champagne.

Anya von Bremzen

Writer-performer BARRY YOURGRAU has been making people laugh their heads off—or gulp in astonishment—with such books as *Wearing Dad's Head* and *A Man Jumps Out of an Airplane*. He's startled everyone with his appearances on MTV and NPR, and even starred in his own movie and in a music video too.

"Now with my *NASTYbook*," grins Barry, nastily, "I invite you to share in those cruel, twisted and shockingly mischievous delights I know you secretly adore—if you dare!"

Barry woke up one day in the United States as a boy. He arrived from South Africa, he claims. . . . Or is this just another of his jokes?

Join in on more Barry trickeries online at www.nastybook.com and www.yourgrau.com.

And oh yes, further NASTYness is brewing! Keep your eye peeled for news of *ANOTHER NASTYbook: Curse of the Tweeties*! (How spooky, how strange . . . what can it mean?)

Hey, is this book upside-down? Or are you?